T0129321

Take Her
and
RUN

GABRIELLA GRACE

authorHOUSE®

AuthorHouse™
1663 Liberty Drive
Bloomington, IN 47403
www.authorhouse.com
Phone: 1 (800) 839-8640

"This is a work of fiction. Names, characters, places and incidents either are the product of the author's imagination or are used fictitiously, and any resemblance to any actual persons, living or dead, events, or locales is entirely coincidental."

Published by AuthorHouse 06/14/2018

ISBN: 978-1-5462-4609-1 (sc)
ISBN: 978-1-5462-4608-4 (e)

Library of Congress Control Number: 2018906829

Print information available on the last page.

Any people depicted in stock imagery provided by Getty Images are models, and such images are being used for illustrative purposes only. Certain stock imagery © Getty Images.

This book is printed on acid-free paper.

Because of the dynamic nature of the Internet, any web addresses or links contained in this book may have changed since publication and may no longer be valid. The views expressed in this work are solely those of the author and do not necessarily reflect the views of the publisher, and the publisher hereby disclaims any responsibility for them.

$\mathcal{D}$EDICATION

This book is dedicated to Clare Braun because it was during one of his sermons that I was inspired to pursue the dreams of my heart. I determined at that time that I would dedicate my first book to him. The dream of becoming a writer has been in me for as long as I can remember, but I needed the encouragement to believe that it was a God-given desire. It still took several years to actually find the time and incentive, but here it is; my first book.

Thanks also to Friends and relatives who offered to let me use their given names for Random characters, and who encouraged me to follow my dreams of becoming a published author.

$\mathcal{I}$NTRODUCTION

This story is fictional; however, as it is based on real people our names have been changed to protect me from a lawsuit and innocent minors from public scrutiny. It started as a daydream, a wish for a better ending to tragic circumstances, but since I've always wanted to write, I decided that this might be the perfect story to put down on paper. I've taken my actual situation and blended it into fictional story in order to write this book. My dream has turned sadness into joy.

Chapter One

What if...

What a beautiful September day! The sky is blue, the leaves on the trees various shades of green and yellow, with a smattering of red mixed in for good measure. They'll be falling soon. Toby, my little terrier and I are walking through the park when I look over towards the swings. My heart leaps into my throat.

It's her! It's Dani!

On the swings, a little girl who looks to be about ten years old is being pushed by a woman in her twenties. The child has her face turned up to the sun, and her tongue is out as if trying to catch the sun's warmth on it. I haven't seen her in three years and know that she is actually thirteen years old now, but I recognize the girl who is stuck with the mind of a toddler.

I freeze, wondering if I should go over there or not. *Would she even recognize me?* I helped to raise her from the age of four until eleven when her dad took her away and refused to let me see her again. He also forbade all school and daycare staff to let me talk to her or her sister.

Toby is still happily meandering around off leash, so I go over and sit on a bench to watch.

"You are my sunshine, my only sunshine..." I begin to sing; not loud, but loud enough that it catches the

1

attention of the girl on the swing. She suddenly plants her feet in the gravel to stop the swing and comes loping over to me at top speed. I hardly even have a chance to get to my feet when I'm enveloped in a huge bear hug. We stand there squeezing one another, neither one wanting to let go.

"Hi, I'm Bridget, Dani's EA," the woman says as she approaches us.

"I'm her mom." I replied, barely able to keep the tears out of my voice. *At least I was her mom for seven of her thirteen years.* The Educational Assistant responds with a smile, "It's nice to meet you!" Apparently, she's new and didn't get the memo that neither I nor her biological mom is to have any contact with her charge.

"How's she been doing in school so far?" I ask as school has just started for the year.

"She's still adjusting to the new school and all," Bridget says. "She didn't want to sit still in class so I took her for a walk and we ended up here."

"She sure does love to swing." I agree.

My mind is spinning. *I wish I could just take her.* Before I could even complete this thought, Bridget suggests it. "Do you want to take her with you?" she asks with a hint of hope in her voice.

"Yes, of course."

"Well, I'll let them know at the school that you've got her. Have a good day!" With that, Bridget walks off.

I was absolutely floored. Excited, elated... and at a loss. *What do I do now?* I wonder. *Can I take her?* Her dad will be furious! I don't know what the plans are for when school gets out, but it's only ten o'clock. I have plenty of time to worry about that. I could spend the day with her and call Gordon later and let him know how I happened to have her.

How on earth I'd managed to get this day off work was a miracle already. What were the chances of running into Dani? This had to be a gift from God. Divine intervention, if you will. What I want to do is to take her and never return her. Thoughts of all the past suspicions and calls to Child and Family Services run through my head. No one is perfect, but some things are just beyond comprehension, in my mind at least. She was an innocent who had been sacrificed to protect her sister, Teri. At least that's my understanding of why the girls remained in a potentially harmful environment, instead of with me, the person who loved and mothered them for most of their young lives.

You're gonna be in loads of trouble, I warn myself. *The longer you have her, the worse it'll be.*

My mind is racing a mile a minute. I've got a few thousand dollars in the bank from a successful summer. Maybe I could go home, grab a few things and just drive and drive and set up somewhere far away. That would mean leaving all my family and friends and my home daycare. It would affect a lot of people. Would anyone understand?

It would mean leaving her twelve-year-old sister alone with her dad. That's the hardest part. I don't know what she knows, if anything, of her dad's secrets. Maybe she's old enough or mature enough, or smart enough to be able to protect herself. Teri is not like Dani, who suffers from developmental delay and can't speak more

3

than a few words. Terri has always been very bright and no matter how bad life is, most kids don't like the thought of leaving their parents.

My hope and prayer is that Teri hasn't experienced nor have knowledge of the things her dad is accused of doing. Without his usual victim handy, would he try to Teri? I'm so afraid that might be the case, but Teri is not here. I have to take Dani only, or no one.

I pray, not so much with words of understanding, but with my heart. What should I do? I wasn't even Dani's biological mom, but I'd fallen in love with her when I first met her. I had been her respite worker…and I'd also dated her dad. I loved both girls, and I spent what time I could with them, even to the point of convincing their dad to let them move in with me. This made it possible for him to accept a job that required him to be at work before daycare opened.

Before long, he also moved in with me, but I could only take about a year of that. I had four of my own kids and two grandchildren living with me already. I needed a helper, but he turned out to be too controlling. It just wasn't working out. Then he went and grabbed my six-year-old grandson by the throat. That was the last straw. I took a chance making him leave. I believed that in order to keep his job, he'd leave the girls with me, and he did. For a time anyway.

By then, I'd started to notice things about Dani. Things that made me wonder. When a child has no inhibitions and can't speak, it's hard to know what is and isn't a warning sign of abuse.

"I never want to leave you again." I tell Dani, and it

sure feels like the feeling is mutual, as her arms are still squeezing me.

"Momma." She says, and I start to weep. She had a vocabulary of about 50 words, last I saw her. I know, as I used to meticulously write down every one. Those seldom used words were also supplemented by a few signs, like "swing". That was one of her favourites.

If I ask Corinne, my assistant, to look after my house and business for awhile, I could go pack some clothes and toys and just head east. I've always wanted to see the East Coast. I can't just disappear and not say anything to my kids, and yet I can't say too much…I decide to call my oldest daughter, Jennifer. She's the one who dyed my hair just yesterday. After being grey for years, I finally decided I wanted a change. *I could pass for Dani's birth mom to someone who doesn't know either of us.* Somehow, I ended up wearing sunglasses, today, too. They would hide the fact that I have blue eyes.

"Hi Jennifer, how's your day going?" I start out with.

"I just had a major cancellation." She tells me. "I wouldn't have come in, if I'd have known."

"Or…maybe you can give me a quick perm." I'm thinking disguises now. I tell what's happened and what I'm thinking.

"Come on in." she tells me and we head there immediately. We spend a few hours at the salon, getting our hair styled and coloured as well as me using my daughter's laptop for checking out camper vans for sale. I've found one just a little way out of Winnipeg. It's not safetied, but I have a good feeling about it and decide to look at it anyway.

A couple of hours later, we leave the shop: two curly headed auburns, and a bleached grayish white dog. Jennifer had decided to give Toby a quick bleach wash on the darker parts of his fur, changing him from a black and gray dog to a mostly gray and white dog.

The guilt comes rushing back. *Why didn't I fight harder to keep the girls together?* I was able to hang onto Dani for much longer. When I still had both girls, I let them see Marianne, their birth mother, which made Gordon very angry. Shortly after this, Marianne contacted me and showed me a letter she had from a social worker recommending that she not let Gordon have the girls because of past allegations. It was this information that gave me the leverage I needed to get Gordon to sign her over to me.

Gordon's oldest daughter, Candace offered to take the girls when we broke up. I argued the idea, but Gordon let her try, anyway. Candace couldn't handle one night of Dani's screaming and ended up calling me in the middle of night to see if she could bring her back. I felt so relieved when custody of Dani was given to me. Unfortunately, it was only temporary. Even with Gordon's consent, the judge only made the court order for 6 months.

I figured Teri would do okay at her older sisters. She wouldn't have to compete with her special needs sister for attention, nor would she have to put up with my two grandsons constantly teasing her. I cried when her dad told me he was letting her go to Candace, but better to her than him. Little did I know it would only last a year. It was a long year, long enough that our close bond was broken. I don't know how Gordon convinced Candace to give Teri back to him. It complicated things in that now he had one daughter again and kept pushing for more and more time with Dani, too.

As time passed and I started working odd hours, it was Gordon having to bail me out by taking the girls more and more. He mostly had Teri, while I had Dani, but we did a lot of sharing back and forth. If only it were a normal situation. I pretended it was. I pretended and pretended, until the evidence was overwhelming and I couldn't pretend anymore.

We soon arrive at the quiet little farm to check out the camper. I examine it inside and out. A couple of seats convert into beds. There's a small table with a couple of bucket seats, a washroom, sink, fridge…all the comforts of home in a tiny package.

"How dependable is it?" I ask.

"Very." The man responds. "We've just outgrown it, with our kids getting bigger and bigger. How far to you plan to go in it?"

I look up at him and decide to spill my guts, "The East Coast. I'm "taking" her." As I briefly explain what I believe has been happening, the owner's wife has come up and overhears our conversation. "That's awful!" she exclaims. They both look horrified at the thought of such a thing.

"Can you excuse us for a minute?" the woman asks. I continue to look over the camper while they walk off to talk together. I open up all the little cupboards out of curiosity and notice that there are still dishes and things inside. The upper bunk would be good for storage.

"We want you to take it," she tells me when they return. "We'll do anything we can to help. We won't even cancel the registration and there's still over a month before it expires."

They ask if I need clothes for her and when I admit that I do, they find some that will fit her. Boy's clothes. They'll work perfectly with her short curly hair. I offer up a silent prayer of thanks.

"Thank you so much! I don't know what to say! You are just an answer to prayer." I tell them. I can hardly keep the tears out of my eyes, and I'm shaking, as well, but I get Dani and myself inside and drive it away. I leave my old van there for them to do with what they want.

I drive back home, but instead of parking in the front as usual, I open up the back gate, so no one sees us, and where it will be easier to load up.

While I'm throwing things into bags, my mind is racing. The past haunting me, but dreams of a future keeping me on track. For the most part, the house is left as is. I call Corinne and tell her I have an opportunity that I can't pass up and could she watch things for awhile as I have no idea when I'll be back. She lives just down the street and is able to pop back and forth as needed. I could leave all the pets, and if I was only going for a short time, I would, but this could be forever. I decide to take the dog (after all, he's now disguised, too), my fifteen-year-old cat and my baby lovebird. The dog and bird are new since my ex and I broke up, so they won't help him identify us. I grabbed supplies for the pets, too. (Good thing I like having surplus of everything.) I tell

Corinne to spend whatever she needs for groceries from the parent's fees. I will work out other details later.

I grab one of my hair brushes, my spare toothbrushes, unopened toothpaste, along with whatever clothes I can cram into a large bag. I then turn to the fridge and cupboards. Crackers, cookies, tins of easy warm up food, margarine, jam, fruit; I'm grabbing food willy nilly as I don't want to have to stop for awhile. I'm wearing a pair of runners, so I add a pair of sandals and a sweater to the few clothes in the bag and we're ready to roll. I still have some of the toys from when Dani was with me, and I grab a few of those.

There is the file folder that held anything to do with custody of the girls, so I make sure I take that. I choose a purse from my collection and make sure I have all my ID, credit cards and cheque book.

Dani, meanwhile, is just wandering around the house. She lived here in this one storey bungalow that I purchased with her needs in mind, for maybe a week, so I don't expect her to remember anything. Although she could walk, if she didn't want to she could make it very difficult as she'd grab doorways and railing with her hands and legs. Stairs could be very treacherous, which is one reason I sold my two-storey and bought this house.

Why did I even move? I had already given her the main floor bedroom in the old house, so I wouldn't have to take her up and down the stairs except for baths. *Money.* I was hoping to buy a smaller house and be able to pay off my credit cards with the profit. It didn't work out that way.

Why did I let her stay with him for the whole week? He'd been taking her more and more to make my life easier. By this time, he had already managed to gain custody back of Teri, so I felt I pretty much had to let him have access to Dani, too.

It takes less than an hour to load everything into the camper, and before I know it, we are on our way. The camper has a glove box full of maps, so we just head east; with me figuring to plot the route in more detail once we stop to rest. I have no idea how I will manage all of that driving. Usually, driving makes me very sleepy. But then I don't normally have the adrenaline rush of a kidnapping to stimulate me, either.

I drive and drive. Dani is a good passenger. Mostly, she just rolls around on the bed. Or she'll play with the toys, pushing the same buttons over and over for hours. I haven't forgotten how to tune out the extra noise. I just listen to the radio or am lost in my own thoughts. I do a lot of praying, too. There are tons of lakeside campgrounds and rest areas in Ontario. I plan to just drive until we need to stop, and decide when we get there how long we'll stay.

In Winnipeg, school is dismissed for the day. Teri gets on the school bus and sits there watching for her sister. Everyone is loaded up and the bus goes to move.

"Wait! My sister's not on the bus!" Teri tells the bus driver.

"Who's your sister?" the driver asks.

"Dani."

"Her aide said she was picked up already."

"Oh." Teri wonders why her dad didn't mention

that Dani had an appointment. *Maybe I'll get some time to myself before they get home.* Now that school has started for the year, it's twelve-year-old Teri's responsibility to look after her sister after school.

Teri enjoys a bit of solitude for awhile before getting bored and lonely. Before long, her dad walks in the door.

"Where's Dani?" Teri asks him.

"What do mean? I just got in the door."

"The bus driver said she got picked up early today. I thought you probably took her to a doctor's appointment or something."

"No." He pushes aside his panic and starts calling various relatives. Tries the school, too, but of course they're closed.

"Veronica wouldn't have her, would she?" he wonders, so he tries that number, too, but there is no answer.

"I guess I'd better call the police." Gordon puts in the call, explaining to them that the child has a developmental level of a toddler and can't speak more than a few words.

After a frustrating evening of pacing back and forth and calling everyone he can think of, Gordon tries my house for the sixth time.

"Hello?"

"Did you take her?" he blurts out.

"Huh? Who is this?" Corinne has just been woken from sleep and hasn't a clue who this maniac is shouting at her.

"Do you have Dani? Someone picked her up from school without telling me."

"I don't know what you are talking about."

11

Corinne and is about to tell him that he must have a wrong number when he continues, "If you have her, you're going to be sorry because I've already called the police." Then he slams down the phone.

"Crazy person." Corinne mumbles to herself, while trying to get comfortable again. Too tired to put two and two together.

Chapter Two

The Hitchhikers

Our first stop is a little campground called Eagle Dogtooth. We hike around for about an hour to burn off my excess adrenaline, and to give Toby some exercise. Dani sticks to me like glue. Not her usual independent self. Maybe it's the uneven terrain. Since we only have a couple of hours of daylight left, we'll camp here overnight. We are not so far away from home that we can't go back easily if I chicken out.

We arrive back and the camper and I want to make a fire, but also have to supervise Dani quite closely. Now that she has her bearings she keeps trying to wander off. We end up just going inside the camper. Once she's occupied with a toy that makes barnyard animal sounds, I turn on my lap top. Using the paper map to plot the basic route, and Google to give me info on the various parks, I try and figure out how far we can get each day.

We will head towards Niagara Falls, taking the longer Canadian route, as I don't have a passport for Dani. If I'm doing all this driving, I'm certainly not going to miss the highlights of the journey.

I check my e-mail - nothing but junk mail. Then I go to my facebook page and briefly scan the postings.

<Hey!> A message from Aubrey pops up. This will be

a test, for sure. Of all people, Aubrey, lives on my street, next door to Corinne. I wonder how much she knows.

<Hey yourself>.

<Kids in bed yet?> I type back.

<No, not yet. What are you doing?>

<Just checking e-mail and facebook. I took Toby for a good walk, now I'm inside for the night.>

<I didn't see your van outside. Did you take him to a park?>

<Yes.> It's tough not to elaborate, as I usually say which park I've visited. I figure I'd better change the subject.

<See any good movies lately?>

<No, you?>

<Last one I saw was Taken 2. It was pretty good.>

<How are your kids doing in school?> Aubrey's daughters used to hang out and help with my daycare kids, while her sons used to help me with other chores occasionally.

<Good. Corinne said that she'll be working for you for awhile. Said she'll have to miss her afternoon classes.>

There it is. The push for information I don't want to give. I would really prefer that people think that I'm still in town, but I guess it's hard to hide things like that from neighbors.

<I'm actually camping right now. Met someone special ;)>
<Oh???>

<Can't say anymore right now.>

<Oh, okay. ☹>

<Well, I've got things to do, so I'd better sign off for now. TTYL>

<TTYL>

Well, I got through that conversation okay. I know I left her with the wrong impression, but I can live with that. I'll have to see if I can change my settings, so that my status shows me as off-line.

After tossing and turning most of the night, I finally get a few hours sleep. I wake up to Dani bouncing on top of me. I groan and cover my head.

"Do we have to get up already?"

I peek over at Toby, and he's looking at me and wagging his tail. He decides to jump up on the bed as well. After hiding my head for a few more minutes, I decide that as there is no way I'm going to get any more sleep, I may as well get up.

After letting Toby and Misty outside, I rustle up some fruit and crackers for me and Dani. Nipper enjoys those, too. The morning is chilly, so we dress up warm and go for a little walk. Misty has done her business and gone back inside. We take Toby and Nipper with us. The sun feels warm and I can tell it's going to warm up fast.

Before heading out, I take a quick peek at the on-line version of the Winnipeg Sun. There is an amber alert out for Dani. I'm suddenly gripped by a sense of panic. *Maybe I should go back?* I take a few deep breaths and whisper a prayer for wisdom. I feel a sense of peace envelope me and I decide to carry on.

I'm barely out of Dryden, when I see some hitchhikers on the road ahead. Looks like a young couple. *Should I or shouldn't I?* I'm so sleepy and it would be so nice to have company, so I stop to pick them up.

Yes, I'm taking a chance, but this young man and woman don't give me a bad feeling, and I believe in trusting my gut. They introduce themselves as Mark and Rachel. Mark just got laid off from his job, so they decided to take some time and travel for a bit. They know people in Quebec City, if they get that far. Although that wasn't originally on my route, I don't see a problem.

"Do you have driver's licenses?" I ask.

"Oh yeah, we both do. Just can't afford the expense of a reliable vehicle." Rachel tells me.

"Well, if you like, you can travel with us. We don't have any set travel stops except for Niagara Falls. I don't have a time limit, but we could get a lot farther if we drove through the night."

"It's a plan!" They seem excited. They just laugh when they see our other travel companions.

"Not only, a dog, but a bird and a cat? That's got to be interesting!" Rachel exclaims.

"And they don't chase each other?" Mark asks.

"If anything, it's the bird that chases the others. He likes to nip at the cats' paws. Misty learned a long time ago that pet birds are not prey."

"How are you guys fixed for cash?" I ask." Are motel rooms and attractions in your budget?"

"Not so much." Rachel replies. "We have some money but want to stretch it as much as possible."

Although, the van can sleep five, if necessary, I'm not sure I'm comfortable sleeping with strangers like that. I guess that's a moot point if we travel twenty-four hours a day. When they are driving, Dani and I can sleep. When they need to sleep, Dani can sit and play while I drive. We can try to work out truck stops and campgrounds for showers. If we do decide we all need a good night's sleep, I'll spring for a motel. If I send them in to pay for it, no one needs to see me or Dani. Most of the parks are deserted, but we occasionally do come across other people. I try to remain calm and cool, so as not to arouse suspicion, but no one seems to take a second glance at our little group of four.

Weather is gorgeous. Not warm enough to swim, but delightful for going on long hikes, or lazing by a river.

The Trans Canada Highway looks to be a good route to get us to the coast. We'll stay on it, unless we find we want to explore any special parks or sites. It's a lot more fun having someone to plan the journey with.

As soon as I get a chance to talk privately, I pull out my cell phone and call Corinne.

"How are things going?" I ask.

"All right, I guess." she tells me. "I got a weird phone call last night and the police came to your place today. They were looking for some girl.

"They showed me her picture. I told them, she wasn't one of our kids." I think they thought I was you, because they didn't even ask where you were."

"Perfect!" I exclaim in great relief. *Maybe things will work out after all.*

"She looked an awful lot like the pictures you have up in your office. What's going on? Do you have her?" She asks.

"The less you know the better." I respond.

"Are you coming back?" she asks.

"I don't know." I reply truthfully. "I can pay my bills and stuff on-line for now." I'm not sure if I can just keep running my daycare at a distance like that, or if

I should authorize my daughter to sell the house and business for me. I'm still winging it here, but as long as people think that I'm still in town, all's well. I'll keep my facebook updated with just basic comments on other people's photos.

※

That night Officer Butler sits up with a start. He thinks back to the pictures he saw on the wall of Dani and others. One picture in particular showed Dani with a couple of boys and a woman with grey hair. But this woman wasn't the one he talked to in the house. He was sure of it.

Butler tosses and turns for the rest of the night. When he goes in to work, he pulls up the driver's license photo of the person supposed to be at the house.

"Oh crap!" he exclaims.

"What?" His partner, Bill comes over.

"She's pulled one over on us. This isn't the woman I interviewed at the house."

"Don't worry about it." Bill tells him." Look what I've dug up on the father. Apparently, people have been putting in complaints of abuse for years."

"Maybe it's just her wanting the kid. That could happen." Dan replies.

"It's been going on long before she came into the picture, although she certainly tried to put in complaints, too. One of his own daughters claims he molested her."

Over the course of the day, they find out that CFS had not only reports and pictures of bruises, but there was an attempt to get Dani examined at the hospital at one point, which never happened.

"I know the younger sister has been questioned before, but I think it's time we took "a go" at her again. Maybe she'll have some answers this time, if she's not too scared to talk."

$\mathcal{M}$Y GIRL

I'm enjoying my time with Dani. Her innocent giggles over the silliest things. Her big bear hugs that nearly squeeze the breath out of me, and so far, no meltdowns. She seems to be happy to be near me. She's not a lot bigger than when I last saw her. A couple of inches taller, for sure. A little heavier. The way she usually sits all hunched over, the beginnings of her female bumps aren't noticeable. I think she can pass for a boy.

Dani follows along contentedly holding my hand when we stop at parks. She sits when I tell her to sit and eats what I put in front of her, for the most part. I'm glad that we mostly eat outside, as she can grab and fling a plate of food faster than you can blink an eye.

One lunch time, I offer her a microwave pizza pop, and she tries to toss that. Normally, she eats pizza pops, I try to make her eat it. All of a sudden, she is vomiting at the table. I guess that means that pizza pops are off the menu. I don't ask her what she wants, as the answer would be chips every time.

I prefer to just offer her a variety of things, and if she eats it great, if not, we'll try again next time. She's always been a picky eater, so I try to serve food I know she likes. She's eating more fruit, I'm happy to see.

Her dad was the one to try to force food on her; his way of making her overcome her sensitive gag reflex. Apparently, she was very difficult to feed as a baby. At three, she was still eating mostly baby food from a jar, but he had a way of feeding her toast and cereal, I didn't like. He would give her a spoonful of cereal, then put a piece of toast in her mouth, too. Sometimes she would gag. Made me feel really uncomfortable. To give her a drink, he would get her to tip her head back and he would pour in some milk from the sippy cup. I guess he wouldn't let her try to feed herself, because of the potential for a mess if she decided to toss it.

Toby is always happy to get out and explore, but is also a very good passenger. I'm surprised how well Misty is taking this travelling. She's hardly ever been in a vehicle, but at 15 years old, I didn't want her to have to adjust to other people taking care of her. The camper is really nice, in that it also has an attached screen tent. If I have to leave the pets for an extended amount of time, I can put them in there. Any other cat, I wouldn't dare let out, but Misty moves pretty slow these days, and if she did try to ramble away, I'd be able to catch her easily. For quick stops, I let her out and she does her business and comes right back. Very handy. I also have a small litter box in the van, if she can't hold it. Nipper has a small travel cage that I put him in, when not directly supervising him. Otherwise, he pretty much has free run of the van. Like the other two pets, he has quite a close bond to me, and I didn't want to leave him behind.

On the road, my new friends and I take turns driving and napping. They seem to be pretty patient with the incessant noise that Dani's toys make, and are fine with the dog, cat and bird all taking turns sitting on them. Nipper, the smallest pet, can be the most irritating. He was a hand fed baby and is used to being around children. This bird has no fear. He crawls all over everyone, and is especially attracted to Rachel's earrings. After shooing him away over and over, he finally gets the message and joins Dani instead. She is sitting in the bucket seat, rocking and humming and playing repetitively with a toy that lights up as it makes music. He's fascinated by the lights and noise. The miles fly by.

We blow through Thunder Bay fairly quickly, just stopping for gas and to replenish our food supply. We also pull into a McDonalds, where I send Mark in with some money to grab us some fast food. Later on, as it's a hot day, we stop at a campground with a lake. Dani heads straight for the water.

"Dani, your shoes! Take off your shoes." I shout after her. She plops herself down, pulls off her shoes and socks and heads back towards the water. She has no sense of danger so I need to follow right behind.

"It's cold!" I squeal, but Dani is already past her knees. She plops down on her bottom, making a big splash, and then gets up and does this again and again. This gives me a chance to get closer, although she gets deeper with each plop. I'm not too concerned, as I know she can hold her breath under water. Soon, she is deep enough that her face gets submerged with the plop. She bounces back up laughing and plops right back down again. I'm glad for my shorts as I'm getting pretty wet. I would have changed into a swim suit if I would have had time, but it's so good to see my baby laughing, I don't mind. Toby's on the shore, watching us. He's not too fond of getting his feet wet, so he'll wait there. I manage to keep Dani from going any deeper, and all's good.

We decide to keep driving. Mark and Rachel can take turns driving through the night. I curl up on the bed with Dani. After trying to sleep with her pulling at my hair and poking my face, I give her an animal sounds toy. Eventually we both drift off to sleep.

The next morning, as we make our way, east, we stop at places that look like they'd be fun for all of us. Mostly parks. There is no shortage of beautiful parks and campgrounds in Ontario and with it being midweek, most places are pretty deserted. I dread Mark and Rachel asking too much about us, or seeing her photo in the paper. I've got my lap top, and keep abreast of the news back home. There's not a lot. There have been pictures of her in the paper a couple of times, but not with her curly red hair. There was an article that listed her birth mother as a person of interest. I hope she stays out of sight, too. Most likely she will, if she thinks the police are looking for her.

The next day, it happens….

"Does Dani have any siblings?" Rachel asks.

"There's a bio sister and various half and step siblings." I answer truthfully. "It's all pretty complicated."

"Where's her dad?"

"I'm pretty sure he's been abusing Dani for years, and yet he's the one who got custody." My eyes tear up as they always do when thinking or talking about this subject.

"That's awful!" Rachel exclaims. "What about her sister?"

"I only pray that he's left her alone. I've always hoped that with him having access to the easier victim, he would leave Teri alone. I couldn't take a chance on trying to find her and taking her. Everything would have just blown up for sure."

Once the floodgates open up, it's hard to stop me and I tell our whole history. Of course, I'm trying not to cry, but that's impossible. I'm soon exhausted and we move on to safer topics of conversation. Nipper has curled up on my neck, and I find that a comfort.

We make it as far as Sioux Ste. Marie, and decide to see what the town has to offer, before we move on to Sudbury. There's a lovely park along the river with a playground. Of course we have to stop there. The canyon tour train ride sounds wonderful, but we decide to opt out as we just don't want to take that extra day. Not to mention the extra expense.

Eventually we stop at a motel, where Mark and Rachel go in to rent a room. We use the showers and hang out with them a bit then flip a coin on who sleeps in the room and who gets the camper. I get the motel room. Dani doesn't sleep a lot, so I like the stimulation of the TV to keep me entertained while she bounces on the bed.

I remember when I used to watch Wheel of Fortune. That always got her interest, but as she would stand right up in front of the TV, it made it difficult to me to see. After a while, I would put it on just for her benefit. She also used to like the weather channel. She was seemingly mesmerized by the words scrolling by along the bottom of the screen.

While in the hotel room, I also try and get her using

words, by playing silly games. I get her to say: "up, down, mom, hug". Not much more right now. But I am delighted that she has made some progress in potty training.

"Pee!" she'll shout when wanting the washroom, or just to go in and play with the light and fan switches. And water. She loves playing with water.

It was a good idea to stop for the night. Now, I can let my pals drive during the day. It's about 6 hours to hit Niagara Falls, but we might want to check out some of Toronto on the way. At least find some dog parks, as it is huge.

As much as I'm enjoying this time, I find I'm ever alert to anyone who might give us a second glance. I call home to get an update on how things are going there.

Corinne answers on the third ring.

"There was a guy yelling and pounding at your door last night around ten," she tells me. "Aubrey heard him and came over to tell me. When he didn't leave right away, I got Robert to go over there. By the time he got there, your next door neighbor was already out there, too. The guys told him if he didn't leave, they would call the police."

"Thanks, I appreciate that," I tell her.

I'm a little worried about this turn of events. It shows that Gordon is still suspecting me and not Maria, the birth mother. I wonder what he'll do next. I decide to e-mail Corinne a photo of Gordon to see for sure if that's who it was at the door. Most of my photos are on my desk top computer back home, but I find one of him on my lap top and send it to her.

Chapter Four

$\mathcal{N}$IAGARA FALLS

It takes us three days to get to Niagara Falls. I find there is a lot more than just the water falls. There's Boat Rides, Butterfly conservatory, Bird Kingdom, even an aero car. We figure we can spend a couple of days on the sites. It's a bit of extra money, but I pay for the four us to visit everything we possibly can. We decide to stay in a motel, when we find one that takes pets.

The walk along the waterfalls is awe-inspiring. Every few feet, Dani stops and gawks, flapping her arms in excitement. We finally make our way along the whole path. We have a couple of even more awesome things planned. We'll take a trip on the Maid of the Mist and take an elevator deep into the falls. There are still the flower gardens, butterfly conservatory and Bird Kingdom. Okay, some of these are more for my enjoyment than Dani's, but I'm sure she'll enjoy them too.

We have a deliriously happy time! I love watching Dani's upturned face as she laughs in delight at the mist spraying on us as we stand on a ledge behind the water falls. The sound is like thunder and the sight is awe inspiring down below Horseshoe Falls. Arms flapping and waving, Dani is enjoying this tremendously. She could stand here for hours, but I'm starting to shiver in the coolness. I try to coax her to leave. "More, more" she signs. We stay as long as we can, then I bribe her to leave with the promise of chips. It's still a struggle.

"We'll see more later." I hug her tightly and pick her up, and begin to carry her to the elevator. Not an easy feat, but Mark offers to help.

"Come, Dani, up! Let's go get some chips now, and then we'll go on a boat ride and see more." Mark coaxes her. She holds on tight while he carries her. In the elevator, she is quivering and shaking her hands to beat the band.

"Someone sure is excited." I smile. "That was pretty cool, wasn't it?"

We find a spot to have lunch, and I make sure there are potato chips, for my Dani.

That afternoon we have a cruise booked on the Maid of the Mist ship and Dani is equally pleased by the water spraying us. She shakes her head and holds out her tongue to catch as much water as she can. I don't care if other people find her odd, I think her innocence and lack of self consciousness is endearing. She is just so precious to me.

An elderly woman smiles at me. The water is pretty loud, but she begins a conversation.

"She's sure enjoying herself, isn't she?" I agree, not noticing that she recognized Dani as a girl and not a boy.

"I've worked with autistic children. They sure are precious, aren't they?"

"Oh yes. The tantrums aren't fun, but it's hearing that laugh that's priceless. It makes life worth living." I respond. I can't help looking at Dani with love and adoration.

When the cruise is over, I'm ready for somewhere warm and we find our way to Bird Kingdom, where we enjoy the hundreds of different birds flying all around us. Of course, I've been "into" parrots for a long time, so that should come as no surprise to anyone that knows me.

I point out the different birds I've had in the past to my friends. "I've had a cockatoo like that one there. She was very sweet, but so destructive. She chewed through window frames, wooden chairs, and once, pulled off all the keys on my computer keyboard. My main problem with her was that she got car sick really bad, and it made it too hard to take her with me any place. I wanted to spend weekends at the lake and do some travelling. I sure hope she's happy, wherever she is."

I see a blue crowned conure. "That's like the first parrot I ever owned, not counting budgies. He just disappeared one winter day. I didn't notice until breakfast in the morning. We had brought in a bunch of groceries the night before, so I don't know if he flew out to meet me and I didn't see him, or if someone stole him while we were out. As I was having breakfast I noticed he wasn't on my shoulder begging for food as usual. I looked everywhere, inside and out. He was just gone. I still miss him. We were so close. He was always on my shoulder. I could take him outside or for car rides and he'd just sit on me. The only time he left was to eat or go potty."

"Cool" exclaims Mark. "I'd love to have a parrot."

"They can be pretty possessive of their favourite person," I go on. "My kids used to leave me a wide berth when walking by, or he'd reach out and snap at them.

I point out the cockatiels. "My nicest bird was a

Cockatiel. Very tame and gentle." Rachel was awed at all of the different colours and types. Blue and reds, yellow and oranges; all so uniquely coloured. And the tricks they could do. Some of the tame ones were good talkers, too.

"Let's get a parrot", Mark says to Rachel, obviously awed by the spectacles before us.

"Depending on the type of parrot, that will only set you back a $1000 or so." I tell him, tongue in cheek. "The better talkers, probably closer to $2000. And then there is no guarantee you can train it to talk, but then some people can even get budgies to talk."

So far, I haven't been able to get my little lovebird to talk, but he's young yet. Also, none of my birds ever really talked, so I don't really have high hopes for that. It's the close companionship that I like. Kind of like a dog, but not quite so big and bouncy.

Bird kingdom done, we are ready to call it a day, so we pick up some supplies for supper and head back to our motel. A couple more sights to see the following day, then we can move on. There's an African Safari only about an hour back the way we came. We'll check that out before continuing our eastern journey.

That night, back in our motel room, we sit and talk. Rachel and Mark tell me about their families. He's the middle child of three. He has an older brother with a couple of kids, and a younger sister, not yet married. Rachel has 4 siblings. She's the oldest. I've only known them a few days, but I'll miss them once we're no longer driving together.

The next morning is Sunday. I'm up early, and I take Dani for a walk around the town. The streets are nearly deserted this early in the morning. We find a park with swings and I push Dani for a while. Quite a while, actually. I'm thinking that maybe I should call home and see how things are going but I'm not going to bother anyone this early in the morning, and I'll probably not find the time later. Oh well. I've been gone less than a week, although it seems longer.

"Let's try the slide, Dani!" I coax her off the swing and help her climb up the ladder for the slide. Once she's pointed in the right direction, she's okay; it's just finding the ladder to start with that's tricky. These new fangled play structures are all made differently, too, but that's half the fun, I guess.

Dani's eyesight has always been a puzzle. Not only does she seem to be near sighted, with astigmatism (wandering eye) but will often trip unseeing over things right in front of her. Her dad used to say that she could spot a bag of chips from across the room, but would trip over the chair right in front of her. That's why I was never sure if the picture cards they made for her at school were any use. With her not talking, it was hard to know what she saw or how well.

After a few slides down, I get her walking again. I have fond memories of when she was at Norquay School; they had one of those bridges that wobbled when you walked on them. She would walk half way across, and then hold onto the railing and say, "Go," and start jumping. Other kids would join her and when they stopped jumping, she would stop, too. Then she would shout "Go" and they would all start jumping again. They would do this over and over, with her laughing with delight as she controlled the play. It was so nice to see those little bits of interaction with other children like that.

Children are so intuitive, too. More than once I would be somewhere with her and a child younger and smaller than her, would refer to her as my baby. I guess they could just tell somehow, that she had the mind of an infant.

As we walk, I make sure to warn her of any ledges or curbs we come to. It's an old habit that I've easily fallen back into. I can't tell if she's gotten better at noticing things like that or not, but I prefer to play it safe, and hold her hand as well.

After a bit, I notice that there are more people around. Hmm a lot of them are coloured people. Then I see that they are entering a little church. I wasn't thinking about attending church with Dani. (I was told at one large church I attended that she was disruptive), but as I walked by and people starting greeting us with a friendly "good morning", I felt that maybe we could try it out. Dani does love music. Even if we just got through the singing, I'd be happy.

We go in and are welcomed profusely. We aren't the only white people, but we are the minority. That alone, makes me feel a little self conscious. But soon, the music and singing start and I'm familiar with pretty well every song they sing, so I join right in. Dani doesn't sing, exactly but I can tell she's enjoying it, by the noises she does make, and of course her big smile. After the songs, the pastor tells people to turn around and greet their neighbour, so we get some more smiles and hellos. There are a lot of children running around, so I feel comfortable enough in the back row to try staying to listen to the sermon. Dani starts bouncing up and down, and I think about getting up to leave. The pastor looks at me as if reading my thoughts, "Don't you dare leave! There's a potluck lunch afterwards." He says with a smile.

I smile back and pull Dani on my knee and rock her while the sermon continues. Aside from a little bit of hand waving silliness, she is relatively still and quiet. After the sermon, we are invited by several people to stay for the potluck, so we do. I figured I'd be crazy to refuse a free meal of home cooked food.

The basement is full of people milling around. Eventually everyone lines up for food. I stack our two plates, putting the food for both of us on the top plate to divide up once I'm seated. People chat to Dani in the way people do when they don't expect a response. I see a boy that looks like he has autism, and another with Down syndrome. I feel more at home, although I am still nervous about responding to questions about who we are etc.

I sit next to a really big lady. I introduce myself using my real name. I will avoid lying if at all possible. I tell her we are visiting the area to see the sights and love it.

"So, where are you from?" she asks. (Of course, she does.) I tell her where we're from.

"You seem a little nervous." She tells me.

"I suppose I am." I say. I don't elaborate.

Other people come up to say hi, asking where I'm from, where I live. Who knew there could be such a difference in answers to those two questions? Usually, the answer would be the same, but as I don't think

I'm living in Winnipeg anymore, it's kind of hard to answer that one truthfully. I just reiterate that I'm from Winnipeg.

I tell about the sights we seen and what we plan to see yet.

"Are you going through the States?" I am asked.

"No, we're just staying this side of the border." They don't need to know that I don't dare try to cross the border with Dani not having a passport. It's added many hours to the journey, but we're managing.

Bang! I jump and turn around.

"It's okay." Another woman tells me, her hand on Dani's plate.

"I just saved his plate from going flying!"

"Oh, thanks!" I respond, noting that she is the one with the autistic boy. She had come to say, hi, and just in time noticed Dani about to toss her plate. I guess there was something on there she didn't like, or else she was tired of being ignored. It can be hard to tell with someone who can't talk.

"Are you all done?" I ask Dani.

"Aw dun" she responds firmly both with her voice, as well as signing. Fortunately, I'm also a fast eater, so have managed to finish my plate as well.

"I guess we should get up before anything goes flying." I say. I get Dani up and we find their washroom before leaving. As we're making our way towards the door the big lady I sat with joins me.

"Is there anything you need?" she asks.

"Just prayers." I tell her.

"Come." She coaxes me into a back room, where I

spill the story. She prays with me right then and there, and I feel better afterwards.

"Thanks so much for everything." I tell her. "I guess we should get going now. We've got a busy day ahead of us still."

That day is filled with us visiting the Butterfly gardens and another view of the falls. Then it's time to head off to our next campsite. We find a place near the African Safari. Being mid September, there is no shortage of campsites. We find one along a creek, and do some wading before it gets too dark. Well, Dani also does some plopping, and ends up getting soaked, but it's fairly warm out, so if she doesn't mind, why should I?

After getting her into dry clothes, I take her to the swing set and push her for a while. It's deserted, so I let Toby off leash. He stays pretty close, until he sees a squirrel, then he's gone like a shot. He doesn't have a lot of staying power, so once it's up the tree he comes back to me.

While we are swinging, Mark and Rachel are gathering wood and getting a fire going to cook some wieners and marshmallows over. Dani is fascinated by the fire. She reaches out as if to touch it, and then pulls back her hand quickly, as if she's gotten burned. I stay alert, just in case. She giggles, and then we start to sing old campfire songs. As we're fumbling along trying our best to remember the words to "On Top of Old Smokey", I hear the strum of a guitar and man with long hair and a beard comes up singing and playing along.

"Thought you mind need some accompaniment," he says.
"For sure."

He introduces himself as Michael and we sing for quite a while, adding a few gospel songs to the mix. Dani gets excited about the guitar and wants to strum the strings. Michael lets her play on it for a few minutes.

I'm getting tired, but Dani looks likes she's still wide awake. I take her inside the van to try and settle her down, leaving our friends chatting by the fire. Mark and Rachel plan to sleep in the screened tent anyway, so they'll crawl into their sleeping bags whenever they are ready. Hopefully, the temperature won't drop too low over night.

I eventually doze off to Dani bouncing on the bed beside me. I wake to Nipper and the wild birds chirping in the morning sun. Dani is still sleeping beside me, so I just lay there contemplating my situation. I feel so happy with her there beside me. I pray for Teri, not knowing how all this is affecting her.

Little do I know that Teri is being interrogated by the police and social workers. Somehow it comes out that there were times at night when she heard strange noises from the room, when her dad was in there with Dani.

"Did you go in there or ask your dad what he was doing?" she's asked.

"No."

"Why not?"

"I don't know. I guess I was scared."

"Are you scared of your dad?"

"Sometimes, like when he gets mad at me."

"Does he ever hit you or Dani?"

Teri just shrugs her shoulders.

"You can tell us the truth, you know. We only want to help."

"I don't want to talk anymore," Teri ends the conversation, and no amount of persuasion will get her to open up any further.

I'm surprised that there is internet service out here, but I check my laptop for e-mail. Mostly just the regular junk, but there is an e-mail from one of Gordon's grown daughters, Candace.

She tells me that she has Teri now, and they want to know where Dani is. She goes on to say that Teri told the police some things and is now afraid to go home.

When I read this, I'm really in a quandary. I don't think it's a ruse, but you never know. Gordon knows how to manipulate people; that's for sure. On the other hand, she's the one who confronted him before. She turned her life upside down to try and protect the girls. Unfortunately it didn't go any better for her than when I tried. I decide to give her a call.

"So, what's happening with Teri?" I ask.

She reluctantly tells me a little bit of what's been happening.

"Do you have Dani or know where she's at?" she asks me.

"I'm not going to answer that right now." I tell her. "The question is, what are we going to do about Teri?"

"She's okay here for now." She answers.

"For how long?" I demand somewhat angrily. "You had her before and let her go back to her dad." If they can't prove anything, they'll just send her back to him, and you won't be able to stop them."

"Well, what am I supposed to do?" she asks, with desperation in her voice.

"Just keep her as long as you can, I guess. Would you be willing to let me take her if we could work that out?"

"I don't know. I love them so much. You do have Dani, don't you?"

"Let's keep in touch." I tell her and sign off.

Chapter Five

DISCLOSURE

It's still pretty early Monday morning, but I can hear Mark and Rachel talking in low voices outside. After spending some time praying for Teri, I join them and we start getting breakfast ready.

"So, Dani's sister has been saying stuff about her dad and she's now at her older sisters." I tell them.

"What kind of stuff?" Rachel asks? I highlight what I know, which isn't much.

"The problem is that the information she's giving isn't specific enough, and they won't be able to do anything for her. This same sister had Teri for a year and gave her back to Gordon."

I'm troubled and happy at the same time. This gives me some sort of hope that maybe I can get both girls together. I have no idea how that would work, as I'm still travelling and don't even know where I'm going exactly.

I make sure my cell phone is on, just in case anyone calls with any new info. No sooner do I go in to check on Dani than it rings. It's my oldest daughter.

"Mom, you'll never guess who just walked into my salon?" she asks. I'm puzzled at first, as it's only 9:30 on a Monday morning, I know her shop isn't even officially open.

"It's Teri, isn't it?" I breathe.

"How did you know?" She asks in surprise

"I've been hearing things. So what is she doing there?"

"She's looking for you. Tracked us down through our websites. She's scared she'll have to go back to her dad, and wants to be with Dani, wherever she is. She packed her backpack with clothes instead of books and snuck out of school shortly after being dropped off.

"Well, can you get her on a plane to…. (I pull out my map) maybe Quebec City or Toronto or…" I rattle of the names of the nearest cities and tell her approximately how many hours I am from each one. "We could even go back to Niagara Falls, if that works out better."

"Okay, I'll check flights and get back to you."

I'm so excited I can hardly sit still, and Dani doesn't help matters As she's bouncing all around as well.

I send a few thanks heavenward, and take Dani outside where I share the news. "Wow, talk about a quick answer to prayer." Rachel comments.

"That's for sure!" I grin. But I don't know if we should just take off now, or do our safari as planned. I have no idea now soon Teri will be on a plane or to which location. We decide that since there is phone service where we are, we'll sit tight for a bit, and do the safari.

The safari is cool. I probably would have gotten more out of it, if I hadn't been so distracted. We did see a lot of animals running free, but it wasn't too much different than a zoo. The animals basically just ignored us. Guess we should have brought along some treats.

While travelling back and forth to the safari, Mark mentions Michael, the guy who joined us at our campfire the night before.

"He's travelling to Charlottetown to be with his mom. Apparently she's getting older and having trouble keeping up with the house repairs and stuff."

"Why isn't he flying?" I ask.

"Apparently his car is crammed full of his personal belongings and his dog."

"Oh, I didn't see a dog."

"It was already in bed for the night."

As my mind is on more important things, I don't give him another thought. I mean, he seemed like a nice guy and all; I just have my mind elsewhere right now.

Meanwhile, back in Winnipeg, Jennifer finds out that there are still a few hours before the next flight leaves, so asks Teri if she wants to go as a curly red head. Teri agrees and they get to work.

"Have you ever been on a plane before?" Jennifer asks Teri.

"No. Are you coming with me?" Teri looks very worried. Well no wonder; she just ran away from home and now someone she barely knows is putting her on a plane to who knows where.

"I really can't take the time. Besides that, I really hate flying." Jennifer's mind is already thinking. Since she was booking the trip in her son, Chris's name already, why not just send her other son, Kevin along for the ride? He was 16 and hadn't yet registered for school after having dropped out the year before. She calls his cell phone.

"Kevin, pack a bag and come to the shop. You are going to visit Grandma." She tells him.

"Why?" he asks.

"I'll tell you when you get here." She adds.

"Is Chris coming, too?" He asks

"Kind of." She responds cryptically. "I'll let you know what's happening when you get here."

He starts to object, but she cuts him off. "Just get over here and bring one of Chris' hats and hoodies. I'm at the shop."

Just then my phone rings and I grab it up.

"Hello?" Its Jennifer's number.

"Well, she can be on a plane to Toronto within the next hour, and will touch down there at 4:05. Oh, and I'm sending Kevin with her. She is afraid to travel alone, and as he's not in school yet, I'm getting him to accompany her. You can keep him for a while, or send him on the next plane back. Whatever you decide."

"Perfect!" I exclaim. "We are on our way."

She gives me the flight info, and I jot it down.

We have plenty of time, but we drive straight through, only stopping briefly just outside of Toronto to give the dog a break. I am so excited. I'm also completely at a loss on how I am going to reconnect with a twelve year old girl that I haven't seen for three years. It crosses my mind that this is all a trick to find out where Dani is, but I can't let my mind go there. We get to Toronto and we still have over an hour, so we explore Central Park for awhile. It's huge! We notice a sign for go carts. That sounds like fun for after our airport pick up.

We get to the Toronto Pearson Airport and park the van. Mark stays with the pets, while the rest of us go in. We may be hard to recognize with the change in hair, but I'm sure Teri will recognize her sister, no matter what. I've managed to see the occasional recent photo of her on facebook, through various relatives, so I'm pretty confident that I'll recognize her okay.

Wow, talk about perfect timing! The plane has just touched down. With no luggage and it not being an international flight, there are no delays to speak of. We wait impatiently at the gate as the people trickle down the ramp. Finally I see her!

"Look, Dani, it's Teri!" I try to point her out, but it's hard to focus Dani's eyes at the best of times, never mind in a crowd of people. Soon Teri is close enough and we move in for a hug! She's not enthusiastic, but allows me to hug her. Dani now has a hold of her and is jumping up and down.

"Your hair!" Teri exclaims. "It's red and curly!"

"Yours too!" I laugh. I introduce her to Rachel, (another redhead) as my travelling companion.

I hug Kevin, too. "Are you going to come with us?" I ask. "We're heading towards the East Coast."

"Cool!" He responds. "I didn't even know you'd left Winnipeg."

"Very few people do. You mom is the only one who even knows where we are right now."

"Well, let's blow this joint." I continue, and we make our way to the exit. I'm still nervous about being seen in a public place like this.

We get to the camper and I introduce her to Mark, and Toby. Of course, Toby is exuberant to meet just about anyone, but I think he helps to make her feel comfortable.

"You have Misty with you!" she exclaims as she sees the cat curled up on what would be her seat.

"Yeah, I just couldn't leave her behind, knowing I probably wouldn't be going back. She's older than you are, you know."

"Really?" She asks. "What about Pumpkin?"

"I left him behind. I didn't think he'd handle travelling so well, as he was still pretty young and energetic." I answer, although, now I'm sort of regretting that decision, as Teri was with me when we picked him out at the Humane Society when she was about 3 or 4 years old. I show her Nipper, the love bird, too.

"You are kind of nuts, eh?" Teri says to me with a smile.

"Oh, yeah, I'm some kind of nuts, all right!" I agree with a big grin.

"I'm so glad to have you here with me, too. I feel so relieved."

I tell Teri a little about our journey, so far. She doesn't say much, but there's no rush. She asks me where we are going and I tell her that I'm not sure.

"I'm sure we'll know when we get there. Just heading for the East Coast somewhere."

"Why the East Coast?" she asks.

"Just because I've never been there and always wanted to see it. For now, there's a go cart place not far from here. You guys want to check it out?" I ask. They are up for it, so we take the carts for a spin. I partner with Dani. She's thrilled. Her laugh is contagious and I laugh along with her. After that, we grab a bite to eat before heading on our way.

We drive for about an hour before I see a place that looks like a good place to stop. It's called Rouge Park, and seems to go on and on forever. We get out and walk around, just burning off energy and exploring woods and streams. It's not easy to keep Dani out of the water. Finally, we find a spot on the rocky shore and I show her how to throw rocks in the water to hear the splash. She throws a rock, listens to the splash, laughs, picks up another rock and does it again and again. Teri, Kevin and I join her for a while, but mostly we just watch and smile. She tries to edge closer and closer to the shore, but I give her warnings and pull her back now and then. Toby lays there with his head on Teri's lap.

"How long are we going to stay here?" Kevin asks.

"I don't know. Once it gets dark we'll be driving through the night, so I like to enjoy the daylight while I can. This will be our last stop today."

"Wow. Do you ever stop anywhere for the whole night?" Teri asks.

"Sometimes, we rent a motel room for the night. But usually we take turns sleeping in the van. It'll be a little more crowded now, but we'll manage. Actually, we'll be in Quebec City before morning, and that's as far as Mark and Rachel planned on going. After that we're on our own, so I'm really glad I have Kevin to help us drive."

We make our way back to our van, where Mark and Rachel have made a little fire and cooked some wieners and beans. The girls aren't fond of beans, so they fill up on wieners with bread. After our late supper, we are on our way again. This time I drive. That doesn't last long. Within the hour, my eyes are getting sleepy, and I ask Kevin if he wants a turn. He hasn't had a tremendous amount of experience yet, but highways are pretty easy, even at night.

He takes over, with me in the passenger seat. The girls are in the buckets, while our other two on the bed.

After a bit, I see that the girls are getting sleepy, and Kevin doesn't look a lot better off. I go back and ask Mark to take a turn, so he and Rachel get up and we all switch places. I put the two girls in the bed, we clear off the top bunk for Kevin, and I lay across the bench seat. It's more of a loveseat, size wise, but I manage.

After dozing fitfully for a few hours, I sense the van pulling in to stop somewhere.

"We're on the outskirts of the city. We can gas up here and we'll sit and have coffee while we wait for a decent hour to drop in on our friends." Mark tells me.

"Okay." I send him in with the gas money and take over the driver's seat. I can see the sun peeking up over the horizon. As long as it's off to the side, it's not too distracting, but I keep my eyes open for good place to stop.

The map shows a park on the other side of Pont du Quebec. I figure if we get out and stretch a bit there, we can then take the main highway to continue our journey. I'll decide the next leg of our journey then. It's really hard to plot a journey with just a map to go by. They never tell the whole story, and even with picking up the occasional guide book, it's still pretty hit and miss. I had no idea before I started on this journey just how big Quebec was, or how close to the coastal provinces it came. It borders on the Gulf of St. Lawrence, which is basically an extension of the Atlantic Ocean.

$\mathcal{W}$ E MEET AGAIN

After crossing the bridge, I drive into a park area. It's still pretty early in the morning, but I don't know how much longer until another nice park. I take Toby and we stretch our legs for a bit. No one else is stirring yet, so I decide to push on to the next place. Halte de Saint-André looks like a good place to aim for. My grasp of French is tenuous at best, but I take that to mean rest stop. It borders Lake Ontario, so it should be nice.

I arrive at Halte de Saint-Andre and follow the driveway around to the lakeshore. This is nice; Lots of trees to wander around in or just walk along the lake. The kids are all stirring by now, so we get out and stretch. I grab us some granola bars, bananas and milk for our breakfast. The kids aren't big breakfast eaters anyway. Of course, Dani wants to run for the water right away.

"Wait, Dani!" The shore is rather rocky and hard to navigate anyway, so that slows her down. We find a place that good for tossing rocks and I get Dani to throw the rocks into the water. We have to throw pretty hard to get beyond the reeds, but Dani has a surprisingly strong throwing arm. Kevin and Teri roam up and down the lakeshore. Toby wanders around, trying to keep an eye on all of us.

"Let's go for a walk in the woods." I call out to the kids. "We have a lot of driving ahead of us."

Only Toby is enthusiastic about the idea, but we go for a hike in the woods. Along the way, we meet a beautiful cocker spaniel. Toby and the spaniel make their doggy introductions and I see the owner coming around the corner. He looks at me kind of puzzled like.

"Veronica?" He asks. "Funny meeting you here!"

"Michael! Yeah! How's it going?"

"It's tough driving all on my own. You picked up some different drivers already?" He asks, seeing Kevin standing there with me.

"Actually, this is my grandson, Kevin. I picked him up in Toronto. And that's Teri, over there." I motion to Teri, who has wandered past us.

"How do you manage to do all that driving on your own?" I ask.

"It's not easy. Michael responds. I drive most of the day, with one stop in the middle. When we stop for the night, I make sure we get some good exercise in, and then in the morning again before we leave." We continue chatting for a bit, as we walk around and end up back at the lake.

I tell him that I prefer driving through the night and spending more time on the sights during the day. Apparently, both methods get us to the same place as evidenced by us meeting twice on the same trip. He seems like a nice enough guy. A bit shaggy with his beard and long hair and all. I remembered the campfire singing. I'm usually a sucker for a guy that can sing, but his shaggy hair and beard remind me of my ex, which is a turn off.

"It sure would be easier if we could all travel together… Wait a minute…I'm going to ask you something. It's okay to say no, but I just remember passing a trailer only a few minutes back. If we drove my car onto it, we could tow it. It would save me gas and energy, and I could help with your gas cost and driving. When I'm driving, the kids could sit in the car if they want. At night, I'd sleep in the car, no problem. I don't want to seem pushy, but I really am getting tired of all this driving alone. I don't mind driving, but alone is pretty hard."

I contemplate his suggestion, and can see merit in it. For one, I'd feel more comfortable with him in the driver's seat, rather than Kevin. With Kevin, I pretty much have to try and stay alert, as he doesn't have his full license yet. Also, having another adult to talk to would be a nice change. The kids haven't been very chatty, so far, although they've been getting better.

"What do you think, Kevin?" I ask.

"I guess so." Kevin replies.

"Okay, sure, I guess we can check it out." I say.

"Great! If you're ready to go, we can meet at the entrance to the park, and you can follow me back to the place I saw the trailer."

It's a full ten minutes before I see Michael's signal lights go on for a left turn. I follow him down the driveway to the house, and we get out of our vehicles. He knocks on the door of the house, and tells the owner we are interested in the trailer they are selling. We all walk over and look at it. It seems perfect, so he haggles them down to one hundred dollars, then he pays them and we hook it up to my camper. He drives his car up and locks the wheels in place. We all climb into the camper and away we go. Michael is driving, and I'm in the passenger seat.

"So do you have your route and stops picked out already?" I ask.

"Pretty much," he tells me, "But I'm flexible."

"That's good, because planning a route has been pretty tricky. I try to Google places up ahead, when I have internet service, but find that is pretty time consuming, and most places are still not what I expect when I do arrive. Fortunately, I'm not that fussy about where I stop, and so far there have been no shortages of gorgeous parks. There's also been a lot more farmland than I expected."

We don't even have that much further to go, but I am starting to get anxious to see the coast. We have our choices now. Keep driving most of the day and night. Or stop more during the day, as we have been. We use the map as a general guideline, but basically just wing it.

We drive quite a while without stopping. Eventually we start getting hungry for more than just the snacks I have in the camper. We are making pretty good time on this journey. Much better than I expected. And I am so glad to have others sharing parts of the journey with me; both as a help driving, and for the conversation. We decide to take the quieter highway along here, closer to the waters of the St. Lawrence. I believe that we are seeing the Gulf of St. Lawrence at this point. We are getting closer to the Atlantic Ocean, that's for sure.

Maybe we should trade in the camper for a houseboat! Wouldn't that be cool! We could travel the rest of the way by water!

As we don't see any houseboats for sale, we take the Route de Montagne to the Riviere Du Loup, then head towards Fredericton. We'll make better time avoiding the city itself.

"What do you say; we stop and eat at a place where we can get a good home cooked meal?" Michael asks me.

"That sure sounds good. We've just been going through drive-thru's, or having picnics." The fact is I still get pretty nervous about sitting in a place where the girls might get recognized. I haven't yet told Michael our story.

Chapter Seven

CONFESSION

Before long, we come across just the kind of place we've been craving, so we stop. After opening the windows to let in air for the animals, we pile out of the camper. We settle into a booth and take turns hitting the washrooms. (We try and use public restrooms whenever possible.) I order roast beef and mashed potatoes. Chicken strips and mashed potatoes for Dani. Kevin and Teri get burgers, and Michael orders himself a steak and baked potato. The booth is a bit squishy with me and the girls on one side and the two guys on the other side. Dani keeps tapping the table as if to say, "Put my food right here."

Our waitress is a well rounded, friendly looking person, named Ruth. She keeps looking at Kevin oddly. I wonder why, but figure as long as the attention is not on the other two, we're good. I was wrong.

Ruth way-lays Teri on the way back from the bathroom.

"Are you okay, dear? Do you need any help?" she asks

"No, I'm fine." Teri responds.

"Are you here against your will?"

"No! I'm not." Teri is alarmed now.

"Your dad is in the hospital with a heart attack. Did you know that?"

Teri shakes her head. "How do you know?"

"I follow the news." Ruth responds

Teri comes back to the table and tells us what she's been told.

"Oh wow!" I respond. "I wonder how your sisters are taking that. I'll message Candace when we get back to the camper."

Our waitress is at the table with our drinks. "Here you go, Maria." She says to me. I almost smile. Obviously, the birth mom is still a suspect.

"Michael looks at me oddly, as if to say, "Is that your real name?" I hold up my hand a little as a sign for him to let it go for now.

"I hope you will use discretion with what you know." I say to Ruth. "You don't have a clue what the whole story is."

"I'm listening." She responds with her hand on her hip.

I take a deep breath. "I raised these girls for 7 years, sharing custody with their dad. When I saw signs of abuse I reported it, but nothing was done except the dad forbidding me to see the girls again. I fought for a while, but I could see that at the very most, only Dani would be taken from him, and I was terrified for Teri, if she was alone in his custody." My eyes are wet and my voice breaks up.

Ruth is visibly shocked, as is everybody else around the table.

"I'll be right back with your dinners. And don't worry. I won't say anything." she tells us, and scurries off.

Michael breaks the silence at the table, "Well that was an interesting story. Is your name really Maria?"

"No, that's their birth mother's name. Apparently

she's still a suspect in this. I had straight brown hair and sunglasses when I took Dani, and said I was her mom."

"I can't wait to hear more of this story." Michael responds.

"It can wait until we're on the road again." I'm impatient to get our meals over with. This sitting around waiting seems like such a time waster when we have so far to go, but I guess it's worth it to get a good meal. Our meals start arriving and we put them away pretty quickly.

Conversation turns to Kevin and why he's not in school. He doesn't say much, so I answer for him.

"He dropped out last year. The school wasn't doing much for him, and he has a hard time focusing because of his ADHD. I was hoping he would register in a school with some good tech programs. He's really smart and mechanically inclined. Maybe he'll stay with me and we'll find a program for him wherever we decide to settle down."

Before long, we're all done eating and Michael asks for the bill.

"Don't worry about it." Ruth responds. "It's been taken care of."

We thank her profusely and head back out to the camper. Misty is at the doorway, so I pick her up and carry her over to a flower garden and let her do her business. The fewer odours inside the vehicle, the better. Toby comes along, but he's not one for peeing every 5 minutes, so he doesn't do anything except sniff around.

We all climb in and get comfortable. Kevin takes his turn driving. Next major city is Fredericton.

Once we are all settled I tell Michael about how I saw Dani at the park, and saw my opportunity.

"So when did you find time to change your hair colour?" he asks.

"My daughter owns a hair salon, and had a cancellation, so I went in right away. I had just done it the day before. I usually don't colour my hair, but I just felt the urge to do it. I really think that God was in all of this."

"Wow." He responds. "And the camper you had already?"

"No, that was another gift from God. It's been miracle after miracle. And even Teri showing up at my daughter's salon a few days later. When she called me, I told her to put Teri on a plane to meet me. Because she was nervous about flying alone, Kevin came along."

"So, you just up and left. No wonder you had to bring all your pets, too."

"It wasn't quite that simple. I left four cats and a thriving daycare back home, but my neighbour has looked after the house and business before, so I've left her in charge until I figure things out. The funny thing there, is that she also has long grey hair, and the police presumed she was me, when they did go there looking for Dani."

"So, your love for these girls is so great that you will risk jail time for them?"

"Well, yeah."

Then I remembered that I was going to message Candace, so I pulled out my laptop and booted it up. First, I go the news sites, to confirm the heart attack story. It's there, so I open up my facebook, and type in Candace's name to open her page.

<Sorry to hear about your dad.> I write.

<Keep me posted. The girls are doing fine.>

I scroll the other postings on my facebook page, and add my comments where appropriate. There's a quote I come across that strikes a chord with me:

<*I'm an idealist. I don't know where I'm going, but I'm on my way. By Carl Sandburg*> It so perfectly describes where I am at right now so I share that on my page.

So, now Candace will know for sure that I have the girls, but will most likely think that I am still in or around Winnipeg. I hate to think bad thoughts about people, and don't hate Gordon, but can't help thinking that if he died, things would go a lot better for all of us. No doubt his children and siblings would mourn his death, but he is pushing 60 after all, and we all have to go sometime. I take a few minutes to pray for his soul. I know that God loves everyone, and offers forgiveness for even the worst sins. That's why Jesus came to die, after all.

I show Michael my facebook page. "This is what I really look like," I tell him. "I don't normally mess around with hair colours and such as I like the natural look."

"I like it too." He tells me.

He's got the natural look going for him, too, but as I said, my ex husband ruined that for me. Now anything that reminds me of him is a real turn off. My ex seemed like a sweet, kind hearted guy who loved children, animals and nature. He was a Christian, too, so that kind of sold it. His religion was pretty strict on a lot of things; no cards, movies, drinking etc. Better too strict than immoral, right? Little did I know at the time but all those do's and don'ts can make a person look good on the surface, but don't necessarily show what's in the heart.

We are so close now. If we kept driving without stopping we'd be there tonight. We'd arrive in the dark, but we'd be there. As it seems a little pointless to drive all that way to arrive in a strange place in the dark, we'll stretch it out a bit. There are lots of trees, lakes and swamp land. It makes for some nice scenery. We find places to stretch our legs here and there.

$\mathcal{A}$lmost There

Michael recommends we find a place to stay for the night around Fredericton. After that, it'll be an easy trek to Charlottetown, and I can figure out what to do from there. Besides whale watching, that is. I'll have to find us a place to stay. Although I had originally been aiming for Halifax, Charlottetown sounds nice, and has the things I've been looking for. At least we do have the camper, so I can also check out the other places before settling down, or after. As I have two children that absolutely should be in school, I will have to get them settled somewhere fairly soon. With Dani, it doesn't matter so much. She is nowhere near her grade level in school. They do what they can with her, but it's not a lot. She stills plays more like a typical one or two year old than a thirteen year old. She would need a program set up before attending.

We are on the road a lot, so I tell the kids since they are missing school, they should make it up by doing some extracurricular activities. They are not pleased with that idea. I quiz them on the multiplication tables, making it a contest to see who can come up with the answer the fastest. As Teri is the more scholarly of the two, it's almost an even match, despite their age differences.

"What's six times six?" I ask.

"Thirty six." Teri and Kevin shout at the same time. "EREE IK" I hear from Dani.

"Dani, did you say thirty six? Good girl!" I exclaim.

"She really did." Kevin says. "Dani, what's five times five?" He asks, but she just giggles.

All three of us try and get her to repeat what she said or try another, but no amount of coaxing is eliciting any other verbal responses. At least it shows she is listening, whether she is grasping what's going on or not. To her, it's probably just a game that she wanted to be a part of.

Another activity I've been getting the kids to do, is journaling our journey. Again, it's Kevin that puts up a stink. He's knows all the excuses: "I don't know what to write. It's boring. I don't know how to spell."

I push him to just write anything. "Describe the scenery. If that's too hard, describe what we are all wearing. You can write down any road signs we pass. Just do what you can."

They have to write it on paper first, as that seems to be a lost skill now-a-days. Later, they can copy it on the computer and they'll have a chance to correct the spelling and edit what they write, if they want. They don't really want, but I persevere. We don't have much else to do. I let them use my laptop for various activities, but no on-line gaming. If they are going to play games, they have to be educational.

Kevin likes looking at the map to determine where we are. I get him to estimate times we will be at various locations.

Candace has messaged me, and I find out that the girls' dad has been released from the hospital with instructions to take it easy. I let Teri know. She seems to feel relieved, but I can also sense that she is feeling guilty for having betrayed her dad. I can understand that.

I talk to my daughter and tell her I want to put the house and business on the market and see what happens. I told her how much money I wanted to get and how much I figured I needed to get, as a minimum. I need to at least be able to pay of my mortgage and hopefully my credit line. Then I will need money to live on for at least a little while, whether I end up renting or buying. I have no idea what I will do for income when I get to wherever I'm going. Probably open another daycare. Now that I have three kids with me, I'll probably need at least a four bedroom house. Yikes! I just have to put it in God's hands, and follow His leading.

It's kind of nice that the money has been coming in, even with me gone. Yes, I do have to pay the helper, but business has been good enough to cover all the expenses. I don't how long that can go on far, as I am the primary person that the clients depend on, and we may start losing them if I don't come back.

We find a campground that is all but deserted and stop for the night. It's a nice spot. There's water and trees. We do some exploring, have some food, and make a campfire. It's pretty cozy, but I am getting a little restless and can hardly wait to be done with all of the travelling. As we sit by the fire, Michael does most of the talking. He tells me about his ex wife, kids and grandchildren. They are mostly in Ottawa. He has a sister in Charlottetown. She has kids and a grandchild living with her.

Michael is a carpenter by trade, and shouldn't have any trouble finding work. Music is just a hobby. He tells me that his mom will hate his long hair and beard, and figures maybe he should shave before he gets there. When he asks my opinion, I tell him he probably would look better trimmed up. I laugh and tell him if my daughter were there, she'd clean him up real good, and probably colour him, too.

"She could colour your hair to match the rest of us, and you'd fit right in like a member of the family." I laugh. Kevin is the only other one in our group with most of his own naturally dark hair colour, but even that has some red streaks in it.

Chapter Nine

ℋELLO CHARLOTTETOWN

The phone rings. It's my daughter, Jennifer.

"Mom, I called a real estate agent this morning and she couldn't believe her ears. She has a client that's been looking for a place to turn into a daycare! She's going to look at it tomorrow. I'll go over there tonight and make sure that things look clean and tidy, and tell Corinne to try to keep it that way tomorrow."

I'm actually in shock when I hear that. It's so sudden.

"That's great!" I say. "What about the asking price?"

"She didn't say anything about it, but I'll keep you posted. How's my Kevin?" She asks.

"He's good. It's good for Teri to have the company of someone closer to her age, too. We're all getting along pretty good, here."

"That's good. How far away from the coast are you?" She asks.

"We'll be there tomorrow," I exclaim.

It's starting to feel real, like this might really be happening. We might be gone from home for good. That's a scary thought. So far from my kids, parents and siblings. That's not what I want, really, but again, I just have to trust in God.

The next afternoon we're in Charlottetown and I hear from my daughter again.

"She's made an offer on the house. It's almost your asking price." She tells me.

"Really?" I can hardly believe this. It's all happening so fast. "I guess I'll take it, then."

"Yes, and she's interested in the contents and just stepping in as soon as possible. By the end of the month, hopefully! I gave her your e-mail address and phone number, so you can work out any other details." Jennifer goes on to tell me.

I'm just flabbergasted.

"Wow, I don't know what to say! That will give me enough money to start over, but I'll sure miss seeing you guys. Once I get settled, maybe I can find enough money to fly you guys down for Christmas or something."

I'm absolutely floored. It's certainly been a whirlwind week. I share the news with Michael and the kids. If I can get the money for my house transferred to my bank by the end of the month, I'll be able start over with little trouble. I hate the thought of being so far from friends and family, but I accept that as the sacrifice I have to make.

I open up my e-mail while we wait for Michael to get a haircut and shave before following him to his mother's place. (We left the trailer at a park outside of town.) He says he owes us a good supper for allowing him to travel with us, and I'm not one to refuse a free meal, so that's our plan of the day. We'll figure out where we are going and what we are doing from there.

There is an e-mail from Kit, the woman who wants to buy my house. She tells me her story: how she has just split up with her husband and he has bought her half of their house from her. She currently works at a daycare and will have to give two weeks' notice, but may not have to work it all out. She's already been talking to her bank and lawyer, and as she already has the money in the bank for the down payment, she doesn't foresee any difficulties with the purchase on her end.

I e-mail back and suggest that if she wants to completely take over by the end of the month, she can try and get to know the parents and children by spending some time when she can by helping out Corinne. I tell her that basically everything in the house can be had for no extra money. All I would need out of there would be photo albums, files etc. Because I have a lot of information on the computer, we can negotiate whether I get someone to transfer all my files off of it, or just take the computer. She prefers to keep the computer. I'll have to get back to her on that.

Then I e-mail my daughter and ask if she can pack up my things. It's mostly the photos I care about. (About twenty albums worth.) There are some files there she can go through to see if there are personal ones that I've missed and also the ones for some volunteer organizations. The files on the children can stay, but I ask her to photocopy the actual business registration forms, so I have a copy. It's tricky doing something like this long distance, but we'll do our best. There are also my tax forms and receipts from the last several years. Kit can always box up things she finds that she doesn't want and Jennifer can pick them up for me.

There is also the issue of the cats. There are still four

cats at the house, and I ask her to please try and find homes for them, unless Kit is willing to keep them. A last resort would be to ship them to me once I'm settled.

After e-mailing Corinne an update on where things are going, I shut down the laptop and wait for Michael. I almost don't recognize him, that's how different he looks. It is a much improved look, and I'm sure his mother will be pleased. I'm just looking forward to a home cooked meal and maybe, just maybe being able to relax on a nice soft couch for a while.

When we arrive at Michael's mom's place, we are greeted warmly. She is the sweetest person! After a delightful lunch of mashed potatoes and ham, we are invited to sit and visit for awhile. The two dogs are minding their manners and not bothering her cat. One warning hiss there was all it took. My cat and bird are still in the camper. It's cool enough with the windows open that they should be fine.

Eventually she offers to let us stay in her home until we find someplace. Dani is sitting on her lap, playing with her necklace. Nicole seems completely at ease with Dani, which causes me to love her even more.

"But there are four of us!" I object. "And that's not counting Michael."

"Oh we can squeeze you all in for a few days, or a couple of weeks. There are still a couple of rooms that can be set up, besides the one I have ready for Michael. Oh, and I won't even be here this weekend."

"What?" Michael asks. "Where are you going?"

"I have a ladies retreat with the ladies in my church. I've had it planned for months. If I'd known you were going to come this weekend, I wouldn't have planned to go, but I don't want to cancel now. It's not like you need me here. We'll have plenty of time together when I get back."

"That's true." Michael concedes. "Well, what do you say?" he asks me.

"It's certainly a tempting offer. And we could always use the camper, too if we have to, maybe for Kevin." It is a big house, and we all seem right at home with each other. Even Teri and Kevin seem pretty comfortable with Nicole. She's just that sort of person.

"Okay." I tell her. "We'll take you up on that, but I'm positive we'll be able to find our own place by the end of the month at the very latest."

"That's settled then." Nicole smiles and shows us around the house. There is extra stuff in the bedrooms, but she gets the guys to haul it up to the attic. The attic is huge, too, and would make an okay bedroom, if it was cleaned out.

"No. I'm not going there." I tell myself. It would be just too weird living in a house with virtual strangers like that. Especially with Michael being a man. No, I'll look for a place in Charlottetown. If I don't find something here, I'll look elsewhere. No problem.

For now, we plan some explorations along the coast. There's a place that good for seal watching. The whale watching cruise is only on the weekends now that summer is over, so we plan that for Saturday.

It's amazing how many light houses there are. There are lovely parks and beaches to visit. Keeping Dani out of the water is a bit challenging at times, but we manage or don't. When we don't, we end up with a cold, wet girl, so I've taken to carrying dry clothes everywhere we go.

Sometimes I have to pick Dani up from behind, by putting my hands under her thighs. It keeps me from getting soaked, if she refuses to walk. I'm careful not to hold her too tight. Someone grabbed her too tight like that once and left a lot of finger marks, causing someone to report that. It didn't click with me where the bruises came from until I saw one of her daycare workers carrying her like that.

As the camper is a bit cumbersome and Michael is still without work, he takes us around in his car. Depending where we are going, we are sometimes accompanied by the two dogs.

At one very nice park, Dani notices someone eating French fries. Oh, oh. She goes over and tries to help herself.

"No Dani. Those aren't yours." I command.

"Sorry." I apologize to the woman.

"It's okay. I shouldn't be eating them anyway." She laughs. "Is it okay if I give him some?"

"Sure." I say. "Dani say please." She makes the sign for please.

"Good girl." I say.

"Oh, she's a girl. I'm sorry."

I'm embarrassed at my faux pas. "Oh, don't be." I respond. "She's not a very girly girl, and prefers comfort over style."

I find out that the woman is a judge. Hmmm, that could come in handy. I remember that I need to get a lawyer to help with the sale of the house, and also to try and get custody of the girls. That one could be tricky, but I want to try and be legal. That would be the only way to feel safe. I'll find one and have a "privileged" conversation, before deciding on my next step.

After a bit of small talk, mostly about pets and animals, we go our separate ways. She seemed nice. Like a regular person. Reminded me of the show, "Judging Amy". I file her name away in my memory bank, until I get a chance to jot it down. It will probably help to get a judge that's already met us. I take some time to make an appointment with a lawyer for Monday.

There are not a lot of houses for sale in Charlottetown, but we start checking them out one by one. Kevin is still hemming and hawing about staying with me. Finally, we come to a nice, big house. It's definitely on the higher end of the possible price range that I can afford. The door is opened by sweet looking middle aged woman.

"Good afternoon. You're here to see the house?" She asks.

"Yes, we are." I tell her. I see the house is still furnished, which is odd, as it had an immediate possession date.

"You seem like a nice family." She adds, as she points out the features of the different rooms. She seems a little anxious.

"I'm just a friend of the family." Michael explains. "They are staying at my mom's until they find a place of their own."

"I see." She responds, then goes on to add, "I was a companion to the lady who lived here. She needed live in help, you see. Her family had money, but no time for her. Well, I shouldn't say that. Very little time. She passed on just two weeks ago, so now I'm looking for a place to stay, too."

"Oh, I'm so sorry to hear that." I tell her.

The house is a split level with a fully furnished rec-room in the basement along with a bar, bathroom, bedroom and workroom. The living area on the main floor consists of a den, living room, dining room kitchen, laundry room, one bedroom and a bathroom. The den has been made into a small bedroom also. The top floor has four bedrooms, none currently in use, but all semi-furnished. It's a wonderful house! I love it! The daycare could go in the basement. Our bedrooms upstairs and we would still have room on the main floor to spread out. I ask about the furniture.

"You'll have to talk to the family." She answers. "I suppose it will have to be sold, unless you want it. They have already been in here and taken some things they wanted.

"What do you guys, think?" I ask Teri and Kevin.

"It's real good," says Kevin.

"I like it," responds Teri.

"If you don't mind me asking, is the little one autistic?" Muriel asks.

"Her official diagnoses are Global Developmental Delay and Seizure Disorder, but she also presents as autistic." I tell her. After trying out all of the furniture, Dani has made herself comfortable on a rocking chair. She seems happy enough, as she rocks back and forth while shaking her hands in the air.

"She must keep you busy." Muriel states.

"She certainly can, and yet other times, she's good as gold and no trouble at all."

"My only child was a lot like her. He passed away a

few years ago." Muriel tells us with a tear in her eye. "I still miss him. It was a blessing when this job came up. It made me feel useful again."

"I don't suppose we could bargain for you to stay on?" I blurt out without thinking.

"Oh, that would be lovely!" I'd be so delighted.

"I plan to turn the downstairs into a daycare, so it would help to have someone to cook and clean and help with Dani."

"Really? You're not joking?" She asks.

"I'm not joking." I tell her. "As long as I can afford everything. I'll need a lot of startup equipment, and the price of the house is pretty high for me already."

I don't even know where to begin. Talking to the owner, first, I guess. Muriel gives me the contact information for Joan Vanderhoof.

"I'll have to talk to Joan first, but don't start packing yet."

"That is so good to hear. It's an answer to prayer!" Muriel blurts out.

I smile broadly. I really believe she is right.

"I don't know how much I can pay you." I tell her. "Maybe a couple of hundred dollars a month to start with. With my last daycare it took a couple of years to actually be profitable."

"Don't worry about it." Muriel responds. "I'm sure we can work it all out."

"I guess that's it for now, thanks for showing us around."

"Thanks for coming."

"Dani, come on. It's time to go." I call. Dani is still

happily rocking. It looks like she will be comfortable here. Teri goes over to her and pulls her up.

"Come on Dani, let's go." Teri tells her. Dani keeps trying wander away, but we scoot her out the door.

No sooner do we get out the door, when I start dialing Joan's number. I'm glad that it's a private sale, and there are no real estate agents to go through.

"Joan? I'd like to talk to you about your house for sale. Can we meet in person?" I ask the person who answers the phone.

"Oh, okay. I'm home right now, if you want to stop by."

"That would be great. Can I get your address?" I ask her.

When we get to the address we are greeted by a vivacious redhead.

"Hi, I'm Joan Vanderhoof. You can call me Joan." She looks surprised to see the whole crew of us.

"I'm sorry to invade you like this, but we've just come from the house." I make introductions: "I'm Veronica. These are my girls, Teri and Dani. This is Michael; we're staying at his mother's house for now."

"Please come in." Joan invites us in.

"We really like the house, and I want to make an offer on it just the way it is. Furniture, housekeeper, everything except any personal belongings you want."

Joan looks quite taken aback by this. Before she can say anything, I add, "You see we had to leave Winnipeg with hardly anything other than the clothes on our backs, and we really need a place to stay." We met Michael on the road and are staying at his mother's until we find a place of our own. I plan to start a daycare in the house for income, as I'm on my own."

"Oh wow. That's really great!" Joan responds. "I felt really bad about having to ask Muriel to move. She's been there for three years now, and doesn't seem to have any family."

"The only thing is the price." I go on. "It's more than double what I'm getting from the sale of my house and business back home. I'd like to make a reasonable offer, and still have some money left to keep us going for a while."

"Well, I'll have to talk that over with my brother, as we co-own it. I'm sure we could come down a bit for the right family. I'll have to warn you about Muriel, though. She's pretty...what you might say...religious."

I smile, "I don't think that will be a problem. Some might call me religious, too." I don't care for the term 'religious' but it's a common term and I let it go. No need to ruffle any feathers and hurt our chances.

Joan takes down my cell phone number and tells me that she'll get back to me soon.

❧

Meanwhile, back in Winnipeg, there's been a new development. Maria, the girls' birth mother, ends up in the hospital. She's been severely beaten up by her husband. Of course the police have to show up to take a statement. They have been alerted that she is a person of interest in the kidnapping.

"So, Maria, how are Teri and Dani doing?" The officer begins.

She looks up at him with a puzzled look on her face. "I don't know." She answers.

"Do you know where they are?" He goes on to ask.

"No, how should I? Their dad hasn't let me see them for years." She replies. "Why?"

"You haven't heard that they've been kidnapped by someone claiming to be their mother?"

"I've been up north. I don't read the papers." Maria responds.

"So, you don't know anything?" The officer asks.

"No. All I know is it wasn't me."

"Any idea who it would be?" He asks.

Maria shrugs her shoulders.

"Do you know who Veronica is?" He probes.

"Yes. She's really nice. She had the girls and she let me see them once, but their dad freaked out." She lies back with tears in her eyes. "I hope she does have them. They'd be a lot better off with her than with that monster."

He continues to question her and finds out that she had became aware of the accusations of abuse by his older daughters. As they didn't say anything until they were adults nothing could be proved. All that happened was that he cut off contact with his accusers.

❦

Back in Charlottetown, I check out the schools in the area and make an appointment with one that seems to have a good record with children with special needs. The appointment is for Monday, so we have a bit of Friday to fill, then the weekend of fun. I think it's time to hit the second hand stores for some new clothes for all of us. Kevin isn't interested, so I borrow Michael's car and just take the girls.

I'm not about to start the girls in school with false identities, so they get all cute, girl's outfits. I grab a few things for myself, too. I also make a note of children's toys and games, but don't want to get bogged down with those until I have a place to put them. I see a couple of keyboards and can't resist grabbing those. Kids of all ages love those. They have a lot of buttons and these ones also can teach you songs by lighting up the keys one at a time. There are a lot of sample songs programmed in as well.

After paying for our purchases, I make my way back to the house without getting lost. Quite the miracle, with my sense of direction. When we arrive back at the house, we can smell supper.

"Mmm. Do I smell food?" I ask.

"Yup, I made meatloaf. I just have to mash the potatoes and we are all set." Michael tells me with a grin.

"Oh, you cook, do you?" I tease. "I'll have to keep that in mind if that housekeeper thing falls through."

We sit down to enjoy the meal, which is delicious.

After dinner, we take our new clothes upstairs. I leave Dani on the couch with one of the keyboards. Teri takes the other one to her room. After putting my new clothes away, I go back downstairs. I'm tempted to wear one of my new outfits, but don't want to waste it, as the day is almost over.

When I get downstairs, I see that Michael is showing Dani what the different buttons on the keyboard do. Or, at least, trying to. She's having fun just turning it off and on to listen to the start up tune.

"The sooner you learn to just ignore the noise, the better." I tell him.

He grimaces. "I can at least try to teach her a tune if she'll pay attention."

"Ah, that's the trick: if she'll pay attention. There's some childish stubbornness, there too, but if you have hours to spend, that's great. She does love music, so I'm sure you could get her to learn something eventually."

Right now, I'm more interested in talking about the new house and chatter excitedly about my plans for it. I hope the lawyers don't drag their feet, as they can with the sale of a house. I remember my last experience of making sure all bills have a final balance that gets paid off. And since the payments had to go through the lawyer the last time, some were late, costing me more money in interest. Not a fun experience. I'm hoping that since the buyer for my house has money in the bank that will speed things up there. And once I have money in my bank, things should go fairly quickly here. Since it's a private agreement, we should be able to cut through a lot of the regular red tape. I sure hope so, anyway.

Michael seems to be excited for me one minute and rather non committal the next.

"My Mom will probably be sad to see you move out." He finally says.

"Don't you think it would be kind of awkward for all of us to stay here any length of time?" I respond. "Besides this place, as big as it is, isn't big enough to run a daycare in and I certainly can't sponge off you guys forever. We're not even related!"

"We could be." He says.

"Huh?" I say, and then see he's blushing. "It would be even worse if we were dating." I tell him. "As long as we act like brother and sister things are fine, but two unmarried people shouldn't be living together."

"I guess you are right. We might have good intentions, but are only human, right?"

"That's right." I agree. I'm glad we've got that settled. I certainly don't have time to even think about dating right now, if ever. Sure, it would be nice to have a guy for home repairs, lifting heavy objects, backrubs etc, but I'm also aware of the statistics of step-fathers abusing step-daughters. It seems that the more vulnerable the child, the more likely to be victimized. A horrible fact of life in today's society.

So many people are naïve to the fact that a little harmless pornography can lead to a sex addiction, and all addictions need to be fuelled with more and more stimulation to get the same high. If it wasn't for pornography, there probably wouldn't be near as many children molested every day.

"Well, Dani, let's go have a bath!" I tell her. I have to take her by the arm and guide her up the stairs. She is still making music as we go. I try and sing along. I learned long ago that music was the key to get her to respond.

Saturday arrives. We spend the morning exploring Central Park, then take the dogs back home and grab some lunch before our boat cruise. The cruise is pretty nice. We see a bunch of seals sunning themselves along a beach. After a while, we see our first whale.

"Look, look!" I yell.

"Cool." Kevin shouts. "Can we get closer?"

The captain tries to edge closer without scaring it off. Then Teri points out the dolphins.

"Look over there!" She points. "Dolphins!"

That is even cooler, as they jump through the air and dance on their tails. We are all delighted by their tricks.

"I wish we had something to feed them." Teri says.

The captain explains that feeding them is discouraged, because they can get too aggressive, and make it hard for fisherman to do their job.

It's a beautiful day; sunny and reasonably warm, although I am glad for our jackets, as the wind blows pretty cool on the water. After our cruise, it's supper, then back to the house to make plans for Sunday. I'd like to see some of the other coastal provinces, but there's quite a bit of driving involved, so I'm not sure what to tackle. We still have the camper so maybe we could drive a couple of hours tonight, camp overnight and finish a journey in the morning. We could go to Halifax or there about. That's a 4 hour trip. A lot for one day, but if we break it up, it would be doable. Or if we want to go even further, there's Cape Breton Island. A 7 hour drive would get us to the coast. As that would be as far east as we can go, it's tempting.

Chapter Ten

Shocking New Developments

Then Kevin breaks the news; he wants to go back home. He misses his brother and friends. I know he misses his mom, too, in spite of the fact he likes to give her a hard time and they can clash a lot.

That means that I should see to putting him on a plane Sunday, so he can be back to get registered in school on Monday. I wonder if it was because I made it really clear that he was going to be in school or working full time. Back home, it was easy to skip school as his mom works long hours and there is always a friend willing to skip with him.

Even with his mom not having to leave for work until after he's settled in school, there is still the morning battle to fight each and every morning. I know he can wear her down. I fought those battles with him for many years before he went back to her full time. Getting him out the door on time was a major challenge. He would get distracted by anything and everything, and then end up rushing at the last minute.

Of course, Teri too is nervous about starting a new school where she doesn't know a soul, besides her sister.

I know it's hard, but there's not a lot of choice. I think back to when I had to start grade seven not knowing anyone. All my peers were going to the Catholic school for grade seven. St. Mary's for girls, St. John's for boys. Not that I had a lot of friends. I was pretty much a loner. I remember I did make some good friends in grade 7 after praying about it. We stayed friends all through high school.

I'm glad I have somewhere comfortable to "squat" while waiting to hear about my "dream house". I keep myself busy checking my face book, and finding out when the next fight to Winnipeg will be. I find that the flight is around 6 PM Sunday. He'll have over an hour at Toronto airport, but that's not too bad. He'll be home before midnight. I call his mom and let her know when to expect him home. I also tell her about the house I'm hoping to get. She's happy her son is coming home.

Sunday we check out some more of Charlottetown. Seems like it will be a nice place to live. Before we know it, it's time for Kevin to be put on the plane. He gets everything packed in his back pack and I see him off. It's been nice having him with me for these few days.

Monday is cloudy with the threat of rain. It's a lousy day to be running around, but it would have been worse to have outings planned, so I try to appreciate that fact.

The school takes Teri in right away, but of course, they have to have all Dani's records and make sure they have an EA staff person hired first. They also recommend that she get an updated physical, as my medical records are pretty out dated.

I left Teri there with a pen, a couple of notebooks and

instructions on how to get back to Nicole's afterwards. I take the supply list with me. I'll have to squeeze in a little shopping along with the rest of my errands.

I'll have to start looking for a car, too. I can't be borrowing Michael's all the time. His mom has one but it's unregistered, as she hasn't been driving for awhile. Something had broken down on it, so rather than try to get it fixed, she just left it.

After a long discussion with a lawyer touching briefly on the buying of a house, and more details on the girls' history, I go off to find a walk in clinic. The lawyer also feels that a doctor exam would probably come in handy.

We find a clinic that is not to terribly busy and sit down to wait for the doctor. They have a pediatrician, but as they also have a female family doctor, I request her instead. The doctor listens to my explanations and fears and prepares for the exam.

"I could do a full exam or I could just request the pertinent files from the pediatrician who examined her when you last took her in." She tells me.

"Sending for the files would work." I say and sign for the file request and give her the name of the doctor and clinic.

Dani has already climbed up on the examination table and is moving around to make the paper cover rustle. A simple thing she seems to enjoy.

"How are you doing, Dani?" The doctor asks as she peers into the eyes, nose and throat. "Say ah!"

Dani complies, more or less. Then the doctor moves

to the stomach area and pushes and pokes as doctors are prone to do.

"I think we should give her a pregnancy test, too." She tells me.

I swallow; thinking of my baby being pregnant is too ludicrous for words. I know she is starting to develop a little, but she's still such a baby.

"Wouldn't hurt," I respond, "but I don't know if I can get her to pee in a cup."

"I'll get you a pregnancy test strip. If you can get her to pee, just dip it through the stream." It sounds easy when she says it, but I have my doubts. We try anyway. One thing about Dani, is that she isn't shy or self conscious.

We go into the washroom, and after successfully getting some urine on the stick, I put it in the pass-thru window and go back to the examination room. Minutes later, the doctor comes back.

"Did you see the results? She asks me.

"No, I just put it in the window." I tell her.

"Well, it's showing positive. I'll set up an ultrasound for later this week to confirm it. As I try to absorb this message, the room starts spinning and the next thing I know the doctor is yelling for the nurse and I'm dropping to the floor. I wake to a wet cloth being rubbed on my face.

"Are you okay?" I'm asked.

"I'm okay." I respond and they help me to sit up. "Do you really think she is?" I ask.

"Her womb feels enlarged, which is why I suggested the test." She tells me.

"Wow. At least I'll have something to tell the lawyer

that we can take to the judge." I respond, while trying to comprehend this latest development.

Errands done, we go back to Nicole's, where I sit morosely, not thinking, not feeling, just sitting. Nicole comes in the room.

"How did things go?" She asks.

"She's pregnant." I respond.

"Who?" She asks "Not Dani?"

"Yes." I whisper, and then break into tears.

Teri and Michael both come in around the same time and give questioning looks. Nicole shakes her head and they wander off.

Finally, I compose myself enough to decide that I need to let their sister know. I grab my laptop and open up the e-mail.

<Candace, I just had Dani at the doctor's and apparently she is pregnant. She has an emergency ultrasound scheduled for Wednesday to confirm how far along she is.>

That's all I can type. I am so freaked out. One of my own daughters had a baby at 15, but that was different. She was normal, had a boyfriend and everything. She didn't have the intellect of a one year old.

I also send an e-mail to my new lawyer, advising her of the latest news. I don't know how I will tell Teri.

Supper time comes and we all sit at the table. It's pretty quiet. I ask Teri how her day at school went.

"It was okay. I met a girl named Ming who is really nice. We sat together at lunch."

"That's great!" I smile. "Do you want to get the school supplies after supper?"

"Okay." She goes on to describe some of the teachers and her classes.

Before, I can ask, Nicole volunteers to watch Dani for me.

"That would be great!" I say. "I haven't been out of that kid's sight for over a week, and it's about time."

After supper, I take Teri and we go and get some school supplies. We try not to take too much time, as she also has homework to do. On the way back, I want to broach the subject of Dani, but I'm not sure how. Finally Teri asks about the doctor's appointment.

"So, how did it go today at the doctor's?" Teri asks.

I take a deep breath, and then let it out slowly.

"The doctor thinks that she's pregnant."

"Oh." She stares at me for a second with wide eyes, and then drops them to her lap.

"She's having an ultrasound in a couple of days to find out for sure, but she thinks so."

Teri just stares out the window for the rest of the ride home. I can't think of anything to say either, and can barely see the road as my eyes are starting to tear up again.

When we arrive back at Nicole's, Teri runs straight up to her room.

"I guess you told her." Nicole says to me.

"I'm sorry." Michael adds. "What now?"

"I don't know. I guess it's the evidence that we need to keep Dani out of his custody, but it might not be enough to protect Teri. Not in Winnipeg, anyway." Yes, there is still some bitterness there, although I've been trying for years not to let it take root.

I'm getting impatient to hear from the owner's of the house I looked at. Finally the call comes in.

"I'm sorry." Joan begins, "but my brother doesn't want to come down in price. He says he could move into himself rather than sell it that low."

"Oh." This is something I hadn't even considered. I don't know what to say. The thought crosses my mind to ask about renting it, but I don't. I feel all choked up again. "Okay."

"I'll let you know if he changes his mind." Joan tells me and signs off.

Now, I'm feeling even lower, like I'm drowning. I can't even really pray, that's how numb I feel. I spend the evening mindlessly watching TV. After getting Dani to bed, I go back to watching TV. At one time, I could never fall asleep to TV, but that all changed when I lost the girls to their dad. I used to cry for hours at night, not able to sleep, so I'd finally turn on the TV and zone out as best I could. I would eventually fall asleep with the TV on. At least I got some sleep that way.

Wednesday comes and with it the ultrasound appointment. I'm terribly tense, and Dani must sense it, as she's been acting up all day. Finally we are in the room, and she's giggling like crazy as the technician glides the machine over her gelled up belly. I watch the screen. They are much more detailed than when I last had one. Even I can make out the beginnings of a small baby. Mostly head, but there are legs and arms, too. I'm completely in awe.

The doctor calls me on Friday morning to say that she's seen the results and estimates that she's about 2 months along. Although, I think I'm prepared, it's still hard to hear.

"You know, it's still early enough…" the doctor begins.

"No." I say. "No abortion. I start to doubt myself. How can I let this child have a child? But it's a baby, I argue with myself. I saw it with my own eyes and love it already. I can't let it be killed, just to make life easier. I also know that abortion is a painful experience and can't put my child through that. Better to just let nature take its course. Of course, I'll be happy to raise the baby.

I shake my head again. "No abortion. We'll keep the baby."

She sees the determination in my eyes and lets it go.

"Thank you." I say. She recommends we come in monthly for awhile before she transfers Dani to a gynecologist.

After I hang up, I e-mail Candace, and call my lawyer with the results.

A little while later, I hear from Candace. She confronted her dad, and he ended up in the hospital again. I'm glad. There are no words to describe how I feel about that creepy little pervert.

On a happier note, I find that the sale of my house has gone through, and the money should be in my account by the end of the day. Monday at the latest. Things were getting pretty tight, as all my savings were about spent, so I feel a lot better about that. Although, nothing can erase the deep disappointment I've been feeling.

I breathe a prayer of thanks to the Lord, but can feel

the conviction that I should be forgiving and praying for the soul of Gordon. That is so hard, but I know it's the right thing to do. I'm aware that forgiving someone doesn't excuse them; it only frees up my heart to accept the forgiveness God offers all of us because of the sacrifice of His Son, Jesus.

"Forgive us our trespasses as we forgive others." It's right there in the Lord's Prayer and how can I say I'm a Christian if I don't follow His commands. I start by praying for God to help me to forgive and ask forgiveness for me harbouring resentments, not only for Gordon, but others in Winnipeg that I turned to for help and who ignored our plight: The CFS workers, the Hospital, the Children's Advocate, The Child Protection Centre; specifically the Director, Dr. Fickleson, who I talked to personally on the phone, begging for an immediate examination. As I'm praying to forgive each one of them, I'm crying, of course, but I start to have a breakthrough and really mean it. I end up by praying for Gordon's soul. I know he had been abused by his father. I don't know how far it went, but abuse is abuse, and it affects people and helps to shape them as individuals.

I don't know how long I've been praying, but I do begin to feel better. I still carry some heaviness in my heart, but the hate has lifted and I try to be positive about it all. I adore babies, so that's not the issue. I certainly plan to keep and raise the baby. But Dani is so tiny. I don't know if she can even carry a baby to term or if she can deliver it. At least, I also have Teri to help out. That's if everything works out for me to keep the girls.

The lawyer has gotten me an appointment before

the judge that I had met in the park. I have to wait until Wednesday, but that's actually a pretty quick wait time. I'll have to plan some fun activities for the weekend, to keep my mind off the waiting and worrying. Maybe another boat cruise, or if it's warm and sunny enough, we can go to one of the beaches and dig for clams. Not to eat. Just for the fun of it.

One thing that I'm not into is seafood, and that is a major part of the PEI Culture. Almost all the restaurants specialize in seafood. Clams and lobster are abundant, but I won't touch either one. But, hey, as long as there is a McDonald's in town, I'm good. I seldom eat anywhere else, anyway. Their price, convenience and child friendliness won me over years ago.

We keep busy over the weekend, attending various festival activities, checking out lighthouses and visiting beaches. By the time Sunday night arrives, we are exhausted, and sleep well.

Chapter Eleven

$\mathcal{M}$ORE UPHEAVALS

Monday morning arrives and I call the school. They still haven't been able to find an EA for her. I ask if I can apply for an EA position there. I do have experience after all. They hem and haw, but finally agree that I can apply. I have to apply for the required Child Abuse Register and Police Records checks. It has to go through the school board as well. I get a call later that day that I can start the following week. They'll put me with Dani to start with, until the checks come through. That way, we can all adjust to the school situation. The other staff will get to know Dani, and I'll get to know the other staff and children I will be working with. It sounds like a win-win situation to me. I'll get an income, and the hours will work out perfectly.

That evening, I get a call from Joan, the part owner of the house I've been trying to buy. They've agreed to rent it to me for a while, but they are not sure for how long. The price is a little high, but I take them up on it. The money has come through from the sale of my house, so I run over with a cheque for the deposit. Then I find out that the pets are not allowed. Not any of them. That's another hard blow to my fragile psyche. I decide to keep looking. I have another week until the end of the month.

Now that I have a job lined up and Kevin gone, I don't need quite so big a place. Funny how things work out.

❧

Back in Winnipeg, Corinne has gotten a phone call from Maria, the girls' birth mother. She wants to talk to me. She left a number, so I call her back.

"Is Maria there?" I ask the person who answers the phone.

"Who's calling please? She asks. I tell her and soon I'm connected with Maria.

"Hi, I'm in a shelter." She tells me. "I heard someone took the girls, and I figured it was you. I want to leave my husband, but I'm scared."

"You need to be strong," I tell her. "You need to get as far away from him as you can."

"Can you help me?" She asks. I don't know what to say.

"I'm a long way from Winnipeg, and right now I'm staying with some people. I don't even have a place of my own."

"I've been going to church, and trying to stay clean. It's really hard."

"I'm sure it is, but I'm not sure what I can do." I don't know Maria very well, but I do know that she has a history of drinking and doing drugs. Sometimes, I've wondered if Gordon deliberately got her pregnant and kept her on drugs in order to have a brain damaged child that would be easier to take advantage of.

"I don't know how long I can stay here." Maria adds.

"Stay as long as you can. I'm not ready to let anyone

know where I am, yet, but I'll call you if I figure something out, okay?"

"Okay, thanks."

"Wait!" I tell her. "I'm going to see a judge about custody the day after tomorrow. It would really help to have you sign off on that. Maybe you could write something up and send it to me. It should be signed by a lawyer, too, probably. Or, if you came here…." I'm thinking now. "Would you be willing to get on the next plane here? You would have to have your ID."

"I can do that." She tells me. "I have my ID with me."

"Okay, I'll talk to my daughter about getting you on a plane. I'll call you back a soon as I can."

I'm about to call my daughter when I get a call. It's Candace. "I have a signed letter from my dad giving you custody of both girls." she tells me.

"What?"

"I went to the hospital with a lawyer and made him give up permanent custody of both Teri and Dani to you. It was either me or you, but I figured since you had them anyway, it might be easier. This way you would be free to come back, too."

"Wow, this I gotta see in person. Can you scan it and e-mail it to me, or maybe drop a copy off at my daughter, Jennifer's hair salon?"

"I'll do both." she tells me.

"Okay, I was just going to call her anyway, so I'll get back to you. How is your dad, by the way?"

"He's not good, but I wanted this cleared up in case he did pass away."

"Thanks, Candace. I can't imagine how hard all this is for you."

Next on the agenda is calling Jennifer. Or should it be looking up flights? I decide to look up the flights first, so I'll know where we stand, time wise. Once I get that taken care of, I call Jennifer.

I make arrangements for her to be at the shop to receive the letter from Candace, then she can pick up Maria and take her to the airport with the letter. She also prints out the flight ticket. The next flight is not until noon the next day. She'll arrive here around 6 PM. I figure she can stay in the camper. Otherwise, I'll get her a motel room. We'll figure things out from there. Meanwhile, I'm back to house hunting.

It looks like we still need a four bedroom. I can't see Maria in a place of her own right away. My head is pounding from all of the information coming at me. I take some pain medication and go soak in a hot bath for awhile. I feel better after a while, and even start to doze in the tub.

Later on, talking to Nicole, she makes me feel better. She's willing to try having Maria stay here with us. Teri can move into the attic. If we find a place that doesn't take pets, she's willing to keep the pets. She is such a warm, caring person, I feel so much calmer after our conversation. She is also still fine with us staying on indefinitely.

Michael comes up with the idea that maybe he should be the one to move out, as he is the only male. He can probably find a small place without too much trouble.

I start to think that maybe I should just go home,

anyway. Continue fighting the battles from there. I'll see what the judge says on Wednesday. If I can get a permanent custody order, I should be in the clear, but you never know with our justice system. They could still try and charge me with kidnapping.

One other little detail, that I almost forgot, is that I no longer have a house to go to. I would have to start over there, too. At least my kids could help me look for a place, since they are there.

I decide to ask Candace to see what she can find out about the kidnapping charge. She can show the police a copy of the letter that Gordon wrote, and see what they say. It's been a long day, and I just want to go to bed.

I hear back from Candace that the police were at the hospital harassing her dad, and he went into cardiac arrest and didn't recover. That stuns me. I'll have to tell Teri. I don't know what her feelings are on all this, as she doesn't talk about it. It's late but I can see the light is on in Teri's room, so I knock lightly. She opens the door.

"Hey, kid, can I come in?" I ask.

"Okay." She shrugs and goes over to sit on the bed. I follow her in, and sit down beside her.

"I heard from Candace, tonight. Your dad suffered a major heart attack at the hospital. He didn't make it."

She looks at me as if not comprehending. "You mean he's dead?"

"Yes." I make a move to put my arm around her.

"It's your fault, you know!" Teri blurts out, and I pull back.

"Yes, I know." I admit. I don't know what else to say.

"I want to be left alone." She tells me, so I go back to my room and pray for God to comfort her.

The next morning, we walk Teri to school and then Dani and I continue to walk around the neighbourhood for awhile. I kind of glad that we aren't too close to the water, as she would want to go it, and it's still a bit cool out.

The walking helps to relieve some of the tension that I'm feeling. It's so hard not knowing exactly where we are going to end up. And taking responsibility for a drug addict might be a little more than I can handle. I'm really glad for Nicole. She makes a good substitute mother.

Thinking of Nicole reminds me of my own mom. I haven't talked to her in weeks. She has no idea where I am, as she's been at Rock Lake for the past while. Although, she just moved back to Winnipeg, I haven't actually seen her yet. How ironic that now she's finally moved back into the city, I've moved out.

My own dad is in a nursing home. I hardly visit him, because it is just too hard. It was okay at first, as he knew me and had lots of stories to tell. It didn't matter that they were the same ones over and over. After a while, he just stopped talking. He would just pace the hallways. At least there is another woman there who also likes to walk the hallways and they walk together. When I'd go to visit a staff person would have to pry them apart, so that we could visit.

The afternoon is sunny and warm so I take Dani and Toby to the beach. She just loves it so much. We go to the less populated areas, so the dog running loose has less chance of causing us trouble. It's been about 2 weeks since we left, but it seems much longer. So much has happened already. I still can't deal with the idea of Dani being pregnant, so I don't even let myself think about that.

We drag ourselves away from the beach, so that we can be home for Teri. I prepare a snack for the kids. We'll eat supper after we get Maria from the airport. On the way to the airport I get to thinking that Teri will probably want to go to her dad's funeral. I guess we'll have to figure something out.

Michael takes us to the airport in his car. He drops us off at the doors while he goes to park. I'm not sure if I'll recognize Maria, as it's been a while and I've only met her a few times anyways. But there she is. The small dark haired woman with the black eye has to be her. The bruising goes all the way down her cheek. That must hurt. She also has a cast on one of her arms.

She seems to have trouble recognizing us at first. I guess she wasn't expecting the red curly hair. And the girls would have grown lots since the last time she'd seen them, about 5 or 6 years ago. Finally, she sees us waving and comes over.

"Hi." She says shyly. "You girls have gotten so big!" Unlike Dani, who is small for her age, Teri is actually quite large for her age. Even reversing the ages, they would still look smaller and larger than average.

"Hi." Teri responds back. She looks like she might go in for a hug, but everyone feels just too awkward. Then Dani grabs Maria in a big hug, which of course brings tears to her eyes.

"There we go." I say. "Dani is happy to see you."

Teri finally goes in to make it a group hug.

We introduce Michael, who has parked the car and joined us.

"Any luggage?" I ask, noticing that she only has a small bag with her.

"No, this is all." Maria replies.

"Okay, good, let's go, then." I respond.

When we get home, I mean to Nicole's, we all sit down to a meal of fish and fried potatoes. Joan does her best to make Maria feel at home.

Teri asks about her arm.

"It's only a sprain. I've got some bruised ribs, too, but I'm okay." Maria tells her. "I'm finally done for good. With guys that are abusive They say they will change and they never do. It just gets worse and worse." I agree with her and then we move on to safer topics such as school.

After a leisurely supper, I show Maria to her room. I also show her everyone else's room. Only my room has a TV in it, and it came with the house. I ask for the custody paper she brought, and told her that I've set up a meeting with my lawyer for just before the court hearing, so that she can sign one, too. Court is at 10:00 a. m., so we'll meet the lawyer at 9:30.

"What will I have to say in court?" She asks.

"Just answer any questions they ask, truthfully. It's Okay to tell them that you've struggled with drugs, and that Gordon wouldn't let you see the girls." I tell her.

"My lawyer will explain that I've raised the girls for many years, until Gordon cut me off, too. He'll also explain the suspected abuse and show the evidence. That reminds me…" I pause. I wonder how to word the latest regarding Dani.

"I've taken Dani to a doctor, and…. I guess he managed to get her pregnant before I took her."

I look up at Maria, who looks grief stricken. Her eyes tear up as she just shakes her head in disbelief.

"The pregnancy is what Candace used as leverage to get him to sign her over to me. That, and the fact that Teri is saying she knows things were going on. All that pressure has been sending him to the hospital with heart attacks. He wasn't able to recover from the last episode." I tell her.

"I'm glad he's dead! She's so tiny and innocent!" Maria exclaims.

"I know."

"A baby. What are you going to do with the baby?" She asks me.

"Of course, I plan to keep it," I tell her, "but I haven't really let myself think about it that much."

"I want to help. I'll stay away from drugs, I promise."

"That's great. I'm sure I'll need help." Although I feel like just going to bed, I can't just leave Dani downstairs by herself.

"Do you want to watch some TV? It's in the living room. I need to go back down and check on Dani, anyway."

"Okay." She responds and follows me back down the stairs.

Teri is trying to do her homework and watch TV at the same time. I let it go, as she gets really good marks in school. Maria, Michael, Nicole and I engage in a bit of small talk. Michael is looking in the paper for a smaller place for him to move to.

"I should get a job." Maria, says.

"Not a bad idea." I respond, and Michael hands her the help wanted section of the paper.

The conversation turns to jobs she's done. Mostly just waitressing. I've heard that she's done some street walking, too, but I keep that to myself. Apparently she has a driver's license, too. That's good to hear. I offer to help her put out a resume.

"We can look up restaurants around town here, and if they have websites, we can e-mail your resume. Other than that, you can walk around and just drop copies here and there."

"You might want to wait a few days, and get comfortable first." Joan adds. "You'll want to get to know the area a little bit." She doesn't mention that fact that showing up to a job interview with a cast and bruising isn't going to make for a very productive interview situation.

While the others are all engaged in their various activities, I sneak up to my room for a bit of quiet time. I get pretty tense, when I don't any alone time to de-stress. And with all this going on, I really need to de-stress.

I'm just trying to convince myself to get out of bed, when Teri knocks, and pokes her head in.

"Do you want me to give Dani her bath?" She asks. She's found that she can read a book while letting her sister splash around

"Sure, that would be great!" I enthuse, and then try to curl up to sleep along with some silly re-run on TV. Of course now that I don't have to get up, I feel wide awake. I've already e-mailed updates to those in the know, and forwarded some silly bit of humour to others on my e-mail list. I open up Facebook again and peruse the latest jokes, quotes and pics. Not a whole lot new, since I last checked. An e-mail from a friend, wondering why I haven't been writing much lately. I try to compose an e-mail that sounds chatty without actually saying anything about what I'm doing. I mention that I'm okay, just crazy busy. Finally, I do doze off in front of the TV.

$\mathcal{T}$HE COURT JUDGMENT

Morning arrives. It's a big day here. I'm keeping Teri home from school so that she can come with us, in case the judge wants to ask her any questions. We arrive at the court house in plenty of time, and find that my lawyer is already there. We chat for a bit. I introduce her to Maria, and they talk a little bit.

"Here's a guardianship letter I drew up giving Veronica your permission to have permanent custody of both girls." While Maria looks that over, I give the lawyer the other one to look over. They seem pretty similar. I also let the lawyer know about the girls' dad passing away.

Once Maria signs, there's nothing to do but wait. Dani has discovered that the walls echo, so she is calling out "Ah" and listening the echo over and over. She's not being too loud, I don't think, so I let her be. I hope she's not bothering anyone. And if she is, that's probably a sure fire way to get us to the head of the line, so to speak.

Before we know it, we are asked to enter the courtroom. Due to the sensitive nature of our case, we are the only ones allowed in.

The lawyer presents my affidavit and guardianship application along with the letters.

The judge calls me forward. She has some hard questions. I have answers to each one.

"You reported your suspicions?" She asks.

"Yes, more than once." I respond and told her that other than talk to a five year old Teri, nothing was done.

"I'm surprised you didn't run sooner." She said.

"The thing is, he managed to have Teri with him by the time I knew for sure. And because I had no support, no-one checking Dani to confirm it, I had no leg to stand on. The most I could have done was to try and keep Dani away, but that would have left Teri more vulnerable. I had to leave Dani, knowing what he was doing, but just hoping that as long as he had her, he wouldn't hurt Teri."

"That is just tragic." She goes on. "And now she's pregnant?" She looks over at Dani innocently looking around the room, seemingly totally oblivious to what's going on around her.

"Just to cover all bases, I'd like to talk to Teri privately for a minute. Will you follow me, please?" She asks Teri, and leads the way to her chambers. After a few minutes, she does the same with Maria.

"I think these girls have had enough upheaval in their lives, and since everyone seems to be in agreement, I'm granting you, Veronica, full and permanent guardianship."

"Thank you. Thank you!" I'm smiling and crying all at the same time.

"I'll try and see that the signed guardianship is ready for you by the end of the week." As the judge leaves, we all exchange hugs.

"We need to celebrate!" I say. I call Nicole to tell

her the good news and we meet up for a simple lunch. It includes both chips and ice cream, so we are all pretty well happy. Except for Teri. I notice that she seems a little down. I guess that's understandable, but I don't say anything. I don't want to touch a nerve and get her crying or anything.

We get Teri off to school in time for her afternoon classes, and Michael takes the rest of us out for a drive. The scenery in Charlottetown is beautiful and Maria is suitably awed. Then we are back at the house where Nicole cooks up some chicken and fries, with chocolate cake for desert.

Nicole is doing really well for someone who is nearly Seventy years old. No major health problems and apparently loves to cook. I'm glad that she has Michael back with her, but it makes me long for my own family. I can't help feeling that I've deserted my own kids by leaving town like this. Sure, they are all adults, but your child is your child forever.

I've burned some bridges there by selling my house, but it wouldn't have been big enough anyway. Not as it was, anyway. I figure as I already have a job here; it makes sense to stay at least for a while. I decide that I should do the year, anyway and then figure out the next step. I don't know. Maybe I can get my kids to look for houses there, and I can look for houses here, and see where I find a place.

That evening I go to check in on Teri. She's just sitting there red eyed.

"Are you okay?" I ask.

"Is he in hell?" She asks me.

"I prefer to think that he's asked God for forgiveness and is in heaven now. Most people do when they know their time is near."

"Even after all that he did?"

"There is no sin too big for God to forgive. That is why Jesus let himself be crucified on the cross. It was to take all of our sins, past and present and future on Himself. The bible says in John 3:16; 'For God so loved the world that He gave his only begotten Son, so that whoever believes in Him should not perish, but have everlasting life.' None of us is perfect enough in our own power to make it to heaven."

"I want to go to his funeral." She says.

"Of course." I reply. "I'll find out from Candace when it is."

Michael ends up finding an apartment for now. They are hesitant about allowing his dog, but he convinces them, by saying that the dog will stay at his mom's except for at night when he's with it. I feel rather awkward pushing him out of his mother's house like this, but he seems okay with it. He'll drop Lady off in the mornings when he's working, and then join us for supper, and just use his place for sleeping. It's a pretty inexpensive apartment, so I guess it's all right. At least he has his own space. I have a hard time getting Nicole to accept room and board for us, but she finally does.

He's found a job already. A couple of them, actually. One is part time, mostly weekends, and the other is full time days. He starts that one on Monday.

Monday is here before we know it. Both Michael and I starting full time jobs, and with me close enough to walk to work, I don't need a car. Maria's elbow still hurts, but she's determined to ignore it and find something as soon as she can.

I'm not trying as hard to find a new place, as I've gotten pretty comfortable at Nicole's. I've got someone to cook and clean and help with Dani. What more could I want? She likes that pesky little bird, too. Lady and Toby get along well, and Misty, well…Misty spends most of her time up in my room on my bed. I have her litter box across the hall in the bathroom, as she doesn't seem to be able to make it all the to the laundry room where Roscoe's is. She doesn't do the stairs very well either, so I keep her food and water in my room. And now that there isn't a man in the house at night, I feel more comfortable sleeping with my bedroom door open. In fact I keep in open all day and night, except for the odd occasion when I just need a bit of privacy. That's why I'm surprised when Misty starts wetting my bed. I get tired of that pretty soon, and make up a bed for her on the floor. It might be age related. After all, she is 15 years old. Then I notice that she's not eating; at least hardly anything.

I guess it's time to make an appointment at the vet's. I get a 4:30 time slot, so I can go after school. When I get there, I make sure I tell the vet to consider her age before recommending a battery of tests. The vet gets what I mean, and suggests that we just put her down so that we don't prolong her suffering. It's hard, but I agree. After driving her half way across the country, it comes to this. At least it's better for her to be with me, so that I know her end is peaceful. I would hate the thought of some stranger just tossing her out in street in frustration. It leaves me feeling rather melancholy, but death is, after all, a part of life.

I remember back to when I first fell in love with tortoiseshell cats. My aunt had one on the farm. The long black, orange and white fur was just so beautiful. Ever since that time, I'd wanted one. I spent years scouring want ads looking for one like it. The closest I came was a female cat named Bruce, a short hair who was predominantly white with a bit of black and orange. Bruce wasn't fixed, so I thought maybe she'd give us a baby more in line to what I was looking for, and she eventually did. Only instead of being black and orange, Misty was grey and cream with a bit of white. She made a very adorable kitten, and grew up to be a beautiful cat. We had a dog at the time that just loved the kittens, and afterwards added birds to the mix, so she was used to being with other animals.

$\mathcal{N}$ow What?

I hear from Candace that the funeral is going to be on the Saturday of the Thanksgiving weekend. I am actually quite thrilled about that, because I didn't think I'd get to see my kids on Thanksgiving, but now I have an excuse to fly in. I book a room at a Canad Inn. They have a swimming pool and a buffet restaurant. What more could we want? Once we check in, I call up family and friends and then we head to the buffet for some supper before spending the rest of the evening at the pool.

The next morning, Candace picks up Teri for the funeral. I had thought of going, too, but ended up feeling that it might be better for me and Dani to stay back. With the possible animosity towards me and Dani's inability to sit still and quiet, I figured we might not be so welcome. I let Candace know, that if anyone wants to come and visit with Dani at the hotel, they are more than welcome to.

All three of the girl's sisters stop by later with their partners and children. They spend some time in the pool with the girls. It's nice to see them all having fun.

Later on Candace confronts me. "When I got my dad to sign that paper, it was so you could come back here with the girls, not stay way across the country."

"Oh, well...It's not like it's permanent." I tell her. "But we do have a place to stay, the girls are in school and I have a job I just started, too. Since I've already sold my house here, I thought I'd stay there for the school year, and then come back."

"You could find a place here, if you tried. I'd really like it if the girls were closer."

"I'd like that, too." I say. After a lengthy pause, I add, "You know, you're right. Since I'm here now anyway, I'll look around. If I can find something by the end of the weekend, we'll just stay."

"I'm excited now, and I open up my laptop to start browsing homes for rent. I figure that would be a much quicker solution to buying."

In no time at all, I have a list of places to check out, and I start making phone calls. No one can say I'm not impulsive! It's not easy to find people home today, but there are a couple that I manage to get a hold of. Only one that is willing to meet me. It's a duplex. Not my first choice, but it has a back yard and the owner is willing to show me the place. I ask Teri if she wants to come along.

"Teri, do you want to look at a house with me?"

"You mean now?"

"Yes. If we find a place to live, we can stay here in Winnipeg!"

"What about school, and...Never mind. Yes, let's go."

"Candace, do you want to stay with Dani, while I check out the house?" I ask.

"Sure. We can stay for a few hours."

"Okay, we'll go get changed, then I'll leave you my room key." I tell her.

While I'm changing I remember that I don't have a vehicle here. I could call a cab, but I'll see if Candace will lend me her car. When we get back to the pool, where Dani is still laughing and splashing with her cousins and sisters, I ask, "Oh, Candace, as I don't have a car here, do you think I could borrow yours?"

"Sure." She tells me and we exchange cars keys for hotel room key.

The house actually looks pretty nice. A brick front and a large fenced back yard. The inside is in good repair, too. One bedroom and a bathroom on the main floor and three bedrooms upstairs. I think that I'll give Dani the main floor bedroom, so as not to have to climb her up and down stairs.

"Just the two of you?" The land lady asks.

"No, I have another daughter who is developmentally delayed."

"Are you working right now?" She asks.

"Well, I have a job, but it's in Charlottetown. I would have to find work here. Probably as a Teacher's Aid. That's what I'm doing there." I use the more commonly used phrase, as not everyone is up on the newer term; Educational Assistant.

"Charlottetown?" She is looking doubtful about taking a risk on such a flighty person.

"It's a very long story." I tell her. "Winnipeg is my home and my family are all here. I just took a trip out there and decided to stay for awhile, so I sold my house in Winnipeg, but now I want to move back."

"I'll need first and last month's rent, plus a security deposit." She tells me.

"That's no problem. I brought my cheque book with me." I made sure I had copies of all my important documents with me when I left, and they stay with me in my purse.

As my mind goes back to Charlottetown and what I still have out there, my thoughts turn to the pets. I had planned on just leaving them in Joan's care for the weekend.

"What about pets?" I ask.

"Do you have any pets?" She responds.

"Well, I left my dog and bird in Charlottetown. Plus I have a couple of cats here in the city that people have been looking after for me."

"I don't like dogs messing up the yard." She tells me. "A cat would be okay, if it doesn't wreck the place." It looks like I'll be asking Nicole to keep Toby and Nipper. That puts a damper on my excitement.

We sign off on the paperwork and I get the keys. I'll have to start searching for furniture right away. I don't want to buy all new stuff, but in order to get delivery of all the heavy furniture we would need, that might be the only way. Then I remember Gill's, a place near my old house. They sell new and like-new furniture and they deliver. It's not far from where we are, so we head over there.

Teri and I pick out bedroom suites, some basic living room furniture and a dining table and chairs. The more I buy, the more I think of. We'll need sheets for the beds dishes, food. I grab a pen and paper out of my purse, and make note of all the things I think of. I make arrangements for a Tuesday morning delivery of our furniture and pay with a credit card.

Now for the other stuff. Although there are stores right along Selkirk Avenue where I could pick up household stuff for cheap, I resist paying for parking if I don't have to. I decide to drive to the Bargain Shop on Main Street instead. They should have pretty well everything we need, including some basic groceries.

Heading down Salter, I see the used car place where my son got his latest car. A light bulb goes on in my head, as I turn the car around. I'm thinking, *Why should I fill up Candace's car with a bunch of stuff when I can fill up my own vehicle.* (Too bad I left my van at the farm; I could have used that about now) Anyway, I pull in to the lot and we look at cars and mini vans. I consider downsizing to a sedan, but there is probably still going to be times when I'm driving more than just the three of us, so I opt for another van.

After putting that down on another credit card, I rush over to the nearest Autopac agent and get it registered. Now I have two cars in my care and control. I call Candace and get the okay to leave hers on the street right by the used car place, and I take my new minivan to go shopping. After loading up on the basic household goods, we head back to the CanAd Inn.

They've ordered a couple of pizza's for supper, and are eating when we get there. Teri joins in, but I hold back, until someone invites me to have some.

"Thanks." I say. "Do you want me to pitch in?"

"No, that's okay," they tell me. Teri and I tell them about the house we just rented and van we purchased.

I let Candace know that I will take her to get her

car when she's ready to go, but one of her sisters offers to do that instead.

It's time to make a phone call to Nicole.

"Hi Nicole, How's it going?" I ask.

"Everything is just fine here. How about you?"

"You'll never guess..." I begin.

"Oh, I think I can guess." She tells me. "I was just sitting here thinking about you, and it came to mind that now that you are back home, you will probably want to stay there."

I'm flabbergasted. "You're right. I already found a place to stay and everything."

"You know what? I'm sure it's for the best. Not that I won't miss you all. I still have Maria, and the pets. You're going to leave the pets here right?"

"Yes, I pretty much have to. The new landlady doesn't want us to have dogs or birds."

"That's not a problem. I'll take good care of them," she tells me. "I'm happy for you."

Now, I'm really glad that Misty did pass away when she did. At least I was with her until her last breath. She was with me from the day she was born, until the day she died; some fifteen years later. I know she was only an animal, but animals are God's creatures too, and also have feelings.

I'll certainly miss Toby too, but the funny thing is I got him mainly to fill the hole in my life when I lost Dani. Now, that I have Dani back, that hole is filled, and I feel like I'm just tossing him aside, and that's not really the case. Nipper is still young and adaptable, so he should be okay. I have to be thankful that Nicole is such a caring person and I know that she will be good to them.

I have a good Thanksgiving Sunday with all of my kids, and my two grandsons. After supper we hang out a bit and chat. Of course, they want to hear all about my trip, so I tell them about the different places we've seen. It occurs to me that now I'll be able to post the photos on Facebook. YAY!

Later, my grandson's ask if they can go swimming at the hotel, so I take them back with me. Their mom can pick them up later.

My mom is planning her dinner for Monday. I'll get to see most of my siblings then. I would take Dani and Teri, but they are invited to one of their sister's places, so they'll go there. If they are holding resentments against me, they are hiding them pretty well, in the interest of peace and harmony. I'm glad, because I certainly don't want to have issues with the girls visiting family members. It crosses my mind at times that they could just try and kidnap the girls, but I don't dwell on that thought. As long as we are getting along well and they can have visits, everything should go okay. After all, I do have a guardianship order signed by a judge, as well as both parents' written permission.

My daughter, Jennifer has reminded me that I have stuff in her storage locker, so I take some time on Monday morning to check that out. There are almost a dozen boxes and bags. Many of them are just from tidying up the laundry room before showing the house to the prospective buyer. The boxes are filled with games, craft supplies and what not. Then there are the photo albums and wall photos, too. The bags contain most of my old clothes.

When I have some time, I scour the ads for EA positions. In addition to getting the girls back in school, I'll have to find work. Hopefully, I'll get a job as an EA so that my hours and holidays with coincide with the girls'.

Tuesday morning we check out of the hotel and drive over to our empty house to wait for the furniture to arrive. The bags of kitchen items that we bought are unloaded into the cupboards. The rest of the stuff waits in bags on the floor and counter.

Finally it all arrives and the men carry the things in. I direct them as to what goes upstairs and what stays downstairs. As we are putting things into place, I realize that I don't have any tools at all. The kitchen table needs to be put together. Pretty much everything else is in one piece already. I run over to the landlady's place and ask for a screw driver. She comes over with it and helps me put it together.

I've found time to call the school. As it's the same school the girls were already registered in, they can start tomorrow. I wonder whatever happened to the EA that I met in the park that day. I wonder if she still works for them, or if they let her go after that incident. Presumably they have someone either on staff or on call that will take care of Dani. I plan to take my resume in, too. Even if I don't work directly with Dani, it will be helpful to be in the same school. We won't have to worry about school buses etc.

Wednesday morning arrives and I take the girls to school. Teri is in grade 7, Dani in grade 8. It's not quite like grade school, where the children are all smaller. These are young teens, and I worry a bit about Dani. When I bring her in, I take a few minute to introduce myself and tell them about Dani's pregnancy. They seem quite shocked, but I assure them that her health seems fine so far. I sense some mixed feelings about that. On one side they want to help, and yet they seem concerned about having a pregnant girl in the school.

"Why don't you have her get an abortion?" I'm asked.

"I don't believe that I have the right to kill a baby!" I answer aghast that they would say something like that to my face.

"It's not really a baby, yet." The principal tries telling me.

"I've seen the ultrasound. It is a baby." I argue. I wonder if this school is the best place for us, but I let it go for now.

The principal also drops the subject.

"Well, let's just get her settled into her classroom. I'll page her EA."

"By the way," I tell her. "I'd like to put in my resume for an EA position. I've got experience with children with special needs and think it will be easier on everyone if we are at the same school."

"We usually find it better to not have parents working at the same school their children go to."

"I understand that, but could you try me out anyway? I could start as a substitute."

"Well, we have some subs already, but we'll see. The application actually has to go through the school board."

"I see. I'll also apply at other schools, but if I get on somewhere else, we'll probably have to get Dani to take the school bus back and forth, so that I'm not late for wherever I'm working. Either that, or I'll move the girls to where I'm working."

I'm not getting a warm, fuzzy feeling at this school, but I will drop my resume at the school board office after stopping at their previous school and asking some of the staff there for recommendations to add to it. I'll apply there also, but if I did get hired, I wouldn't be able to transfer the girls over as it only goes up to grade six.

I'm not too concerned about a job, yet. In fact I'd like to get our routines established and make sure that Dani is settled into school okay first. I can do a bit of volunteering there, too.

The rest of Wednesday is filled with picking up a few more essentials and talking to people who might write a reference letter for me. I called my friend, Taundra, who I've worked with on Community volunteer boards. I get her up to speed on what was happening:

"What?" Taundra exclaims when I tell her that I have gotten custody of Dani. "No wonder you missed the last meeting. How did I not know what was going on?"

"Sorry, but I had to keep things hush-hush when I first took her." She's even more flabbergasted when she hears the whole story.

"You kidnapped your daughter, took her to the East Coast and back, and I'm only hearing about this now?"

"Considering that it all happened in the space of a few weeks, it wasn't hard to keep it all under wraps. Not even my own mother knew what I was doing." I tell her.

"Wow! You should write a book about it all! Taundra tells me.

"Yes, maybe I should! Only I don't think it would be believable enough! I laugh and ring off assured that she'll supply me with a good reference. I also stop by Norquay School, where all my kids went at one point.

At the school, there are still a few people working there that know me as Dani's mom. I let them know that I have regained custody of both girls and am now looking for work as an EA. After a bit of catch up on how well the girls are doing, I leave with the promise of a few more references. A lot of people have trouble following through with things like that, but I hope to get at least one out this trip.

Last of all, as I have forty-five minutes before the girls are due to be dismissed from school, I decide to stop by my old house and say hi to the kids there. I drive over there and knock on the door. Boy does that feel weird! Kit answered, with a couple of little ones surrounding her legs. (Good, I didn't wake them up from their nap.) I almost expected to hear the dog barking, forgetting for a moment that he was miles away in Charlottetown.

"Veronica, Veronica!" They squeal, as they embrace my legs.

"Hi there, sweeties." I say, as I bend down to squeeze their little toddler bodies. I look up to Kit and introduce myself. "I'm back in town, and just had to stop by and say hi." I tell her.

"Oh, okay. I'm Kit. Do you want to come in?"

"Just for a couple of minutes." I say, as other little heads are peeking out from the nap room.

"Veronica's back!" One of them exclaims, and before I know it, I'm being smothered by more hugs.

"How is everything going?" I ask Kit.

"Things are going well. We've gotten to know each other pretty good."

"Are you staying home now?" One of the little ones interrupts.

"No. I have another house now. Kit is looking after you now, but maybe I can visit once in a while." I answer. "I'm looking for work, in case you need help." I tell Kit with a grin.

"Oh, you know what? I still have a couple of boxes of things that I decided I didn't need, if you want them."

"Sure. I am starting from scratch here outfitting a whole new house." I tell her.

"Are you going to start another daycare?" She asks.

"No, been there, done that." I reply. "I'm looking for work as an EA now, because it will fit it better with my daughters' school schedule. Their dad had full custody for a while and that's why I could do it before. "I notice the time is flying by and I have to get going, so I gather up the boxes and head out to the van.

"Where's your van?" A little boy asks.

"I have a new one. This blue one over here is my new van." I point to it.

"Wait!" Kit calls. "There's a grey tabby cat hanging around, that I think is yours, but she won't come into the house."

"That must be Hailey. She's always been nervous about strangers." I tell her.

"Look, there she is!" Kit points to a cat peaking around the corner of the house.

"Hailey! Here kitty kitty!" I call. She looks like she

wants to come, but is hesitant. "Can you take the kids in the house, so I can try and grab her?" I ask Kit, and she does. It doesn't take much more coaxing to get her to approach. The poor thing looks half starved. When she gets close enough, I start petting her, then grab her tightly by the scruff of the neck and pick her up. I climb stairs and tap the front door with my foot. When Kit answers, I ask if she still has the cat carrier in the shed.

"Actually, it's right here." She says as she points over to corner of the porch. "I was hoping to try and trap her."

"Oh yeah, I see it. Can I use it? I don't want to have her loose in the van, in case she takes off and gets lost."

"No problem." Kit tells me. "I'll feel a lot better knowing you have her now. The other ones are doing okay. I don't mind keeping them, unless you want them back."

"I'll call you later about it. I'm running late." I tell her. It's nearly 3:30, so I drive directly to the school. Dani is already waiting outside with her EA.

"How did it go?" I ask.

"We had a pretty good day." He tells me. "We did a lot of exploring the school and went for walks. We also did a little work."

"Good." I don't have time to say more, as Dani is already trying to head towards the van. Once she's buckled in we sit back and wait for Teri. It's not a long wait. As soon as she opens the front door, she sees the cat carrier and peaks in.

"Is that Hailey?" She asks.

"It sure is." I tell her. "I stopped by the old house to say "hi" and managed to grab her. She's been too nervous to go in the house, so I figured I needed to take her back."

"What about the other cats, like Pumpkin?" Teri asks as she climbs into the van and puts the carrier on her lap.

"I figure we can get Pumpkin and Mittens and just leave Tigger with Kit." I answer, as I put the van in gear.

Soon we are on our way back home. I still have bags and boxes of things in the van to take in. Teri helps me bring in the things and we quickly go through the contents. There are some towels, blankets and a few miscellaneous kitchen items, including little used cook books. I find places for everything and start supper.

Tonight it's just chicken strips and potato wedges, but I plan to start cooking real meals. Nicole has shown me how to hide things like spinach and mushrooms in lasagna. I want to start eating as healthy as possible, for the girls' sake. I know they haven't been used to eating a lot of fruits and vegetables, but we've slowly been adding them to our diet. I've never been much of a cook, as I don't like to take risks with food.

Things seem to be going okay for the girls at school. There is one day that Teri comes home and tells me that she could hear Dani screaming during one of her classes, so she asked to be excused and went to help.

"Dani was sitting in the hall and having a meltdown about something, but calmed down when I went to talk to her." Teri tells me. She told me how she got Dani distracted with some gadget, and then she was ok to get up and walk back to her room. "I told her EA that sometimes she just needs to get up and walk around, and if she's not allowed to do that, she'll start throwing things around."

"It's good that your teacher let you leave the class, like that." I tell her.

After supper we make arrangements to pick up the other two cats. On the way, we pick up a few supplies that we'll need, including a spray bottle. I'm nervous about Pumpkin scratching up the door frames of our new place. Rather than cry to go outside, he's always just scratched at the door frames while waiting for someone to open the door. I never did break him of that habit, but I plan to try harder now since I'm only renting.

Now that we've settled in, my thoughts go back to the years that I missed with the girls. I decide to have a belated birthday party for Teri. Her birthday was in the summer. I've missed three of her birthdays, so I make up my mind to buy her three big presents. It's hard to know what to get a twelve year old girl, but I ask what she would like. She's gotten back a lot of her things from her dad's house, so she doesn't really need a lot, but I've noticed that her clothes aren't fitting as well as they should. I think she must have grown a couple of inches over the last month, but her pants are getting looser instead of tighter. Must be all the exercise and healthy food.

Teri invites a few friends over to celebrate and we order pizza. She seems to be making lots of friends at school. I try to get them interested in some games, but they would rather just hang out in Teri's room. That's okay. They are twelve after all.

Dani's birthday is next month, so I can wait to have hers on the exact day. Another month after that and it will be Christmas, so I shouldn't go too wild. It is nice to have money to spend. I've spent many years never having enough. Still, I need to be careful, as it won't last forever. Especially if I keep spending more than I'm bringing in.

I still haven't heard anything from my job applications, but it's only been a few days. I've also applied for more Child Abuse and Criminal Records Checks. Certain jobs they have to been done regularly, other jobs just when you change employment. Not that it's a sure guarantee that someone isn't a child molester. As long as you aren't convicted, you'll have a clear record.

Before long, I do get an interview and then get hired on as a sub. It's not a regular pay check, but it will have to do for now. On the bright side, I do have some free time on my hands. I prefer shopping without the distraction of others, especially if I have to do a full shopping trip. It's really hard to keep track of Dani at the same time as concentrate on what I need to buy. I don't like leaving her with Teri, either, as you just never know what she might do.

When rent time comes up, I suggest to my landlady, that if she's ever in the market to sell, to let me know. I've still got a couple of kids that don't have homes of their own, so a duplex could work. I don't think it would be their first choice to share a place with their mother, but if they were desperate enough, maybe. Or else I could rent it out to two of them, and buy myself something else. Those are just some thoughts I've been having. It would help to have some extra income.

Winter comes and with it snow and cold. I have a party for Dani, and invite her sisters, and any other aunts, uncles and cousins that want to come. We rent a room at a hotel for the night, so the kids can swim. She gets lots of presents. Most of them are clothes, but she gets some toys, too.

I finally get a full-time position in their school I work with a wheelchair bound little girl. Very precious. Although she can't do a lot, I talk to her and read to her, and take her to the different classrooms. Whenever Dani has to miss school because of a doctor's appointment I have to miss as well, so then Dani's regular EA takes over for me.

$\mathcal{W}$ITH EVERY BREATH
I BREATHE

Christmas is just around the corner. Dani has begun showing. I do a lot of playing with baby dolls with her. Show her how to change diapers, hold a baby etc. That becomes part of her school program, as well. Even if she isn't going to be caring for the baby herself, it will be in the house and she'll have to know to treat it gently. I've told her that a baby is growing in her tummy, but it's impossible to know how much she understands.

The thing with people who can't talk is they often have understanding far beyond their capabilities to communicate. A wonderful book that demonstrates this is "Carly's Voice". It's about a girl with autism who cannot speak. After many years of intense therapy she learns to type. Although painstakingly slow she has learned to make her needs known and has been able to explain how well she understands what is going on around her. It's been a real breakthrough on what some people with severe autism may be experiencing.

Anyway, Christmas is fast approaching. I've invited Maria to come and stay with us for a few days. She can have friends or relatives come and visit her here if she wishes as long as she understands that there is no smoking, drinking or drugs allowed in the house. That's as much for her protection as it is for the benefit of the girls. I don't need anyone coming over here to influence her back to her old ways. I also strongly discourage her from attempting to visit others who may tempt her to start drinking again. She seems to have embraced her new lifestyle and we spend a few good days with her. She helps around the house and helps me to prepare the Christmas dinner at my place.

It's a tight squeeze for sure with me inviting my siblings and parents, as well as my children and grandchildren. Hosting big gatherings has never been my thing, but I'm trying to improve. A lot of people aren't sure what to do with Dani, so it's easier to have people to our house. Besides, I've been improving in my cooking skills, so it's a good opportunity to show off. It all turns out well. There is lots of food, fun and presents.

The relatives that couldn't make it on Christmas Day find other times during the holidays to stop in and say 'Hi'. Shopping has been a challenge. I don't like taking children shopping with me, nor am I comfortable leaving Dani for long with anyone. I've qualified for a few hours a week of respite, and I make sure I use that up. My son and his wife sometimes look after Dani for me. They are also expecting their first child for August. I'm absolutely thrilled about that, as are they.

The girls also have some invites to various relatives. Sometimes, I'm also included, so that's really nice. It's good to get to know our extended family better. It's delightful to have that week of rest and visiting. The abundance of holidays is one good reason to work in a school. Working in the same school with Dani makes things even easier.

One day while driving down the street next to ours I see a duplex for sale and check it out. It's a bit small for me, but the price is reasonable. It needs a bit of repair, but I can nearly pay for the whole thing with the money I still have from the sale of my old house. I wonder if my kids would want to rent it from me, if I gave them a good deal. When I bring it up to them, they are enthusiastic, so I buy it. After the sale goes through, I give the tenants three months notice to find other accommodation, so I can make the repairs then rent it out to my own kids.

Winter seems to fly by, what with work, Doctor's appointments etc. We've found a female gynecologist who seems really caring. Another ultrasound shows us the baby is a girl. I mention to the doctor that it would be convenient for the baby to be born during Spring Break, not that I believe that we can rush these things.

"That might be a bit early." The doctor says. "However, if the baby is anywhere around six pounds by then, I'd certainly consider inducing labour. We don't want her to get too big, with Dani being so tiny."

Spring break comes and goes with no baby making an appearance. It is still too early, really, as the doctor figures she's only about four and a half pounds. We do have a whole week with which to go shopping for baby supplies. I resist the urge to buy everything new. I know I have only a finite amount of money and don't want to waste it. Nor do I want to end up in debt or with a mortgage I can't afford.

Easter Sunday is a great finish to a busy week of preparations. I have my kids over for Easter dinner after church. After months of searching, we have finally found a small church not far away where we feel comfortable attending. As time goes on we grow closer and closer to some of the members. Esther and Iris are two unmarried sisters that I become especially close to. Although they've never had children of their own, they are very patient with other people's.

Time speeds by now that it is spring. It's my favorite season, as I just love the longer days and the warmth of the sun on my face. I can hardly wait to start planting some flowers. There are a few perennials I recall from when I first moved in, but I always like to fill in with some long blooming annuals such as snap dragons and anything else that catches my fancy.

April 21 rolls around and I'm woken by odd noises coming from Dani's room. I jump out of bed to go and check on her. She is bent over and groaning. I immediately go over to her and put my hand on her stomach. It is tight, and then relaxes. I'm sure it's the end of a contraction.

"Are you okay, Dani?" I ask, with my hand still on her stomach. She is rocking back and forth, but I feel it; another contraction.

"Teri!" I call. "It's time!" Teri and I scramble into some clothes. I just pull a light jacket over Dani's pajamas, and slip on her rubber boots.

At the hospital, it seems to be taking forever. I'm in the room trying to comfort my "baby" while the doctors and nurses bustle in and out. Dani's doctor has been called and arrives shortly.

Dani doesn't know what to do, and wants to keep getting up out of the bed. We let her walk around a little bit, then get her laying back down again for the next check. I go through my repertoire of little songs that she likes to hear. "You Are My Sunshine" is a favourite. It's not long before she's fully dilated and ready to push.

"The baby's in distress." I hear someone say.

"We'll have to take her now. We can't wait." One of the doctors is saying.

"You should wait outside." I'm told.

"No! Jesus, please help!" I pray

They are trying to put a mask on her face but she fights it. Someone is trying to pull me away, but I refuse to let go of Dani's hand. I put my head on the bed beside hers. I can feel her want to sit up and push, so I help her. The mask slips away as she gives a huge, groaning push.

Seconds later, I hear a weak little cry and sit up. The nurse has a tiny infant in her arms, which she wraps up and hands over to me. I stand up and take her into my arms. She is so tiny and precious! Her cry sounds like that of a kitten.

"Clear!" I hear, as the nurse pushes us further away from the bed. It barely registers, but then I turn around to see they have the paddles on Dani and they are shocking her. Once, twice, three times, before they back off.

"Look at the baby! Look at the baby!" The nurse is urging me. She has her arms around the both of us, and she maneuvers me over to a chair and sits me down. It's all very surreal. I try to concentrate on the tiny bundle in my arms, but I can't help looking over at Dani. Then finally, the flat line on the screen comes to life as Dani struggles and moans. She's come back! She looks pretty played out, but turns her head to look for me. I get up and show Dani the baby.

"Look, Dani! The baby!" I say as Dani weakly reaches over to gently touch the baby's face. I bend over and kiss Dani's forehead. "Good girl, Dani. You did a good job." I tell her as she closes her eyes and drifts off.

"What are you going to name her?" The nurse asks softly, bringing me back to the baby in my arms.

"I don't know. We'll think of something special." I start to cry. My 'forever baby' girl just had a baby of her own. I know my life will be turned upside down, but that's okay. Every child is a blessing and I plan to treasure my little ones with every breath I breathe.

###

Printed in the United States
By Bookmasters